BLACK LIBRARY
CELEBRATION 2018

After you enjoy the stories in this anthology,
we recommend the following titles:

The Horusian Wars: Resurrection
John French

■ Black Legion ■
Aaron Dembski-Bowden

Book One – The Talon of Horus
Book Two – Black Legion

Lukas the Trickster
Josh Reynolds

WARHAMMER AGE OF SIGMAR™

Hallowed Knights: Plague Garden
Josh Reynolds

Overlords of the Iron Dragon
C L Werner

THE HORUS HERESY

A Thousand Sons
Graham McNeill

Scars
Chris Wraight

The Master of Mankind
Aaron Dembski-Bowden

BLACK LIBRARY
CELEBRATION 2018

John French, Josh Reynolds, David Guymer,
Guy Haley, Chris Wraight and
Aaron Dembski-Bowden

BLACK LIBRARY

A BLACK LIBRARY PUBLICATION

'The Absolution of Swords' and 'A Trick of the Light' first published
as eShorts in 2017.
'Bear Eater', 'Pantheon', 'The Last Son of Prospero' and 'Into Exile'
first published as eShorts in 2016.
This edition published in Great Britain in 2018 by
Black Library,
Games Workshop Ltd.,
Willow Road,
Nottingham, NG7 2WS, UK.

10 9 8 7 6 5 4 3 2 1

Produced by Games Workshop in Nottingham.
Cover illustrations by Mark Holmes, Rachel Pierce
and John Michelbach.

A CIP record for this book is available from the British Library.

ISBN 13: 978 1 78496 701 7

See Black Library on the internet at

blacklibrary.com

Find out more about Games Workshop
and the worlds of Warhammer at

games-workshop.com

Printed and bound by CPI Group (UK) Ltd, Croydon, CR0 4YY

CONTENTS

WARHAMMER®
40,000

The Absolution of Swords

John French

'Claims of innocence mean nothing:
they serve only to prove a foolish lack of caution.'
– Judge Traggat, *Selected Sayings*, Vol. III, Chapter IV

I

Snow had come to Crow Complex as night fell. The ice-laden wind spiralled through the stacked domes and spires, reaching its fingers down into the cloisters to ripple the flames of candles. A trio walked through the ragged light, crimson robes dragging over the stone floor. No one stopped them. They passed like shadows beneath the sun. Most of the members of the complex's orders had hidden from the cold as the sun had set. Those few hurrying through the processionals saw the bronze hand of the Order of Castigation hanging around the trio's necks, and moved on. One did not draw the attention of the castigators unnecessarily.

The first of the trio was tall and slender, and the fall of the robes made it seem to glide over the floor rather than walk. Brass glinted inside its cowl. The second was heavier-set, and walked with head bowed and hands folded into its wide sleeves. A checked band of white and black silk ran around the hems of its sleeves, marking it as the abbot of its order. The last was hunched, fat, and moved with dragging steps. The fabric over its shoulders bulged, and it clinked as it walked. A length of chain trailed along the ground beneath the edge of its robe. To anyone considering if they should check the trio's progress, this last figure removed any doubts; a weighted penitent was a visible reminder of the price of sin and the cost of absolution.

The wind tugged at the trio's hoods as they stepped onto the Bridge of Benevolence. A sheer drop fell away to blackness either side of the narrow span of stone. Snow was already settling on the slabs.

'Sweet tears of Terra,' gasped the hunched figure, as a gust cut across the bridge.

The figure in the abbot's robe turned its head slightly towards the hunched figure behind him.

'Your pardon,' said the hunched figure, and then muttered to himself. 'This wind is enough to flay the armour off a tank.'

The trio passed on across the bridge, and towards the looming mass of the High Chapel. Hundreds of metres tall, and over a kilometre across, its size rivalled the cathedrals of other worlds. Twin doors of iron stood closed at the end of the bridge. Plumes of flame rose from vast braziers set to each side of the archway. Copper feathers cascaded down the face of each door.

A pair of guards stepped from niches as the trio reached the end of the bridge. Each wore a brushed-steel breastplate over white robes woven with scarlet flames. Both carried lasguns, the barrels hung with saint coins and water vials. The

Ecclesiarchy had held no men under arms since the Age of Apostasy, so these guardians were technically separate from the priests whose will and creed they followed. They were of the Iron Brotherhood, pilgrim warriors who had taken oaths to guard the chapel's sanctity. Of all the souls in the Crow Complex, they were some of the few who would question the right of an abbot to pass where he wished. They levelled their weapons at the trio.

'Entrance to the chapel is barred by order of the prefectus prior,' said one of the guards. 'I cannot open the way, even to your order.'

The trio stood unmoving and silent.

'By whose will do you come here at this hour?' snapped the other guard. 'You are not Abbot Crayling. Who are you?'

'I ask your forgiveness,' said the first of the trio, her voice sharp and clear. The nearest guard blinked, tattooed skulls briefly closing over his eyes. The other opened his mouth to speak.

The robed woman crossed the gap to the guards in a blur, red cloth spilling in her wake. The nearest guard pulled the trigger of his gun. A fist hit the back of his hand. Bones shattered. He gasped air to shout, as an elbow whipped into his temple. He fell, lasgun slipping from his grasp to the snow covered ground. The second guard was slower, his fingers still scrabbling at the safety catch of his gun as the woman grabbed his collapsing comrade and threw the unconscious body at him. The wind caught the hood of their attacker and the velvet cowl fell back from a slim face beneath a shaven scalp. The second guard toppled, and tried to rise. A boot lashed across his jaw. He slumped to the ground. The lasguns went tumbling down into the abyss beneath the bridge a second later.

'Someone will notice,' said the hunched man. Neither he

nor the figure dressed as the abbot had moved. The woman glanced up at him. The x-shaped henna stain running across her face made her eyes seem like polished jade set in copper.

'I will add it to my penance,' she said, 'but we do not have the luxury of time.'

The fat figure grunted, chains clinking as he shifted his weight. The hunch on his shoulders moved. A slit in the side of his robes opened and a fabric-wrapped bundle slid to the ground.

'If we are abandoning subtlety I won't need these,' he said, pulling chains from under his robe and letting them rattle to the ground. He knelt and unbuckled the straps around the bundle. The fabric peeled back; oiled metal gleamed within its folds. A pair of bolt pistols etched with gold feathers lay beside a long-hafted warhammer, and a sheathed great longsword. Beneath them were ammo clips and a narrow-bladed power sword. He tossed the bolt pistols to the girl with the painted face. She caught them, checked their action and holstered them beneath her robes. He passed the rest out, and for a second the clink of weapons and harnesses chimed against the wind.

The man in the abbot's robe settled the sword behind his shoulders, stepped up to the doors, and pushed a section of the frosted metal. A small door hinged inwards.

'Follow,' he said, and stepped through.

II

'You sleep at the other end,' growled the Pilgrim.

Cleander Von Castellan sighed. He was starting to wish that they had picked a different infiltration location than this forgotten hole.

The cavern he now squatted in had not been made for the purpose it now served. Cleander guessed that it had been a water cistern, feeding the thirst of the first monasteries built when Dominicus Prime had been a barely populated backwater. Now it was a store for the tides of humanity that came to the shrine world. Like everything in the sprawl built by the faithful, it had an acquired name that rang hollow to Cleander's ear. The Garden of Eternity, they called it. Pillars marched into the dark holding up a ceiling of cracked plaster. Crude paintings of trees and vines wound up their sides. Sheets of cloth hung from wires strung between the pillars dividing the cavern into a maze of spaces. The light of small fires and oil lamps cast shadows against the fabric screens. Salt deposits glittered where the rough floor met the bases of columns. Glum, unwashed faces had risen and looked down again at Cleander and Koleg as they had passed. There had been no offers of help or friendly greeting to fellow pilgrims. This was the kind of place that bred despair rather than good cheer.

They had eventually found a place in the maze of screens. That alone had been difficult. Every space had a claim on it, and they had to exchange cylinders of fresh water to find somewhere. The commerce that clung to almost every inch of life down here in the Warrens almost made Cleander want to laugh. They had to pay an offering of candle tokens at three shrines for directions to the Garden of Eternity. When they had found the entrance, it had turned out to be a rusted iron door set in a crumbling arch beneath a sculpture of the Emperor as provider. Even then a hooded crone sitting just inside the door had held out her hand for a donation. Cleander had noticed the blunderbuss welded to the metal struts of the crone's other hand, and handed over another token. That the thug of a pilgrim who loomed over them had some claim on the bit of ground he sat on did not surprise Cleander. It was, though, getting on his nerves.

He looked up into the pilgrim's face. The man's head was a ball of scar tissue arranged around a snarl of broken teeth. Tattered fur covered his shoulders, adding to the bulk of the muscles beneath. Layers of stained cloth covered the rest of his body. Red veins spidered the yellow of his eyes.

Cleander tried a smile.

'I am sorry, brother traveller,' he said. 'Is something amiss?'

The big pilgrim raised a hand and jabbed a thick finger towards the other end of the sleeping hall.

'You sleep down there,' growled the pilgrim.

Cleander glanced at Koleg, but his companion's eyes were focused on a point in the distance, his face as blank as ever.

'We have already paid to be here,' said Cleander, and fixed his smile in place. He could almost see heavy cogs turning in the big pilgrim's skull.

'You go–' began the thug.

'No,' said Cleander. 'Like I said, we have paid.' He held the smile in place, his good eye barely flicking as he sized up the thug. Lots of muscle, arms tattooed with tiny, black dots, one for every day spent on pilgrimage to the Crow Complex, a gang brand from Iago running around the left forearm.

The thug's patience seemed to run out. He stepped back, tensing to lash a kick into Cleander's face. The man's collar shifted down his neck. A circle of faded ink coiled at the base.

'The Tenth Path,' said Cleander quickly. The thug froze. Cleander reached up to his own throat, careful to keep the movement slow, and pulled his collar down. The tattoo was false, but looked real enough: a ragged halo of ink curled around a bare circle of skin. He flicked his eyes at Koleg. The soldier returned the look without expression and bared his neck to show the same mark. Cleander looked back at the thug. 'We are seekers of the Tenth Path.'

The thug looked between them. The other pilgrims sitting nearby had already shrunk back, and made it very clear that they had other things to concern them.

'You,' said the thug at last. 'Follow.' He turned and began to walk towards the far end of the cavern. Cleander stood, lifting the roll of rags holding his possessions and hanging its rope cord across his shoulders. Koleg followed, pulling his coat close about him. The specialist's face was impassive as always, flint-grey eyes moving over the fabric partitions and huddled pilgrims as they passed. Koleg moved with unhurried care, precise and controlled. The dark skin of his scalp glinted in the firelight, the old surgical scars pale lines around the base of his skull. Unless you had spent years in the specialist's company, there was little for the eye to catch in his appearance. Most people tended not to notice Koleg, as though he blended with the banality of life. He was also one of the most dangerous people Cleander had ever known.

They trailed the thug, passing down a corridor between fabric screens. People pulled back from their path, and Cleander could see fear in their eyes in the instant before they glanced away. It was not him that they feared, he was sure. At times he had cowed pirate lords and alien princes, but here and now he was just a man with one eye, a ragged beard and greying hair. Clothed in patched and reeking rags, he looked and smelled just like all of the rest of lost humanity.

'Where are we going?' he asked the thug.

The brute kept walking. 'To see the confessor.'

Cleander felt his gut tighten, but kept his face impassive. A confessor could be trouble. The firebrand priests of the Ecclesiarchy were often dangerous and likely to deal with those they saw as heretics without mercy or waiting for reasons. It had taken him and Koleg three weeks to get this far. They were walking the Tenth Path, down into the dark. Now it might end not in revelation, but in fire.

'Here,' said the thug, stopping and pulling aside a panel of weighted fabric. They stepped through. The base of one of the pillars rose from the centre of the space beyond. Worn fabric hung over the rough stone, threadbare carpets covered the floor, and bowls of burning oil stood on poles. There was no sign of anyone else. The thug let the hanging drop, and turned to them.

'What is the truth of the first path?' he said.

'That there can be truth,' said Cleander without a pause.

The thug looked at him, nodded slowly, and then looked at Koleg.

'What is the truth of the second path?'

'That the universe is truth,' said Koleg.

The thug stared at him.

Cleander held himself still. It had taken a lot of work and more than a little blood to learn the replies they had just given. Those words should be enough to take them one more step, but if the thug asked another question they were in trouble. He felt his fingers twitch, feeling the absence of his digi-rings.

The thug nodded, and moved the hangings covering the base of the pillar. A corroded metal door sat beneath. A heavy lock had been welded to the door and frame. A ragged circle had been burned onto the metal. The thug pulled a key on a leather thong from under his tunic, and slotted it into the lock.

Cleander took a step forwards.

The thug paused, hand still on the unturned key. 'How found you the path, brethren?' he said.

A chill ran over Cleander's skin. He licked his lips, mind racing through all of the intelligence Viola had compiled for them on the Tenth Path. This was not a question that they had encountered. The question might have been one of the cult's ritual challenges, or it might be simple curiosity. Either way there were more wrong answers than right.

'By many steps, brother,' said Cleander carefully. There was an extended moment in which he held the thug's stare. The man's gaze twitched.

Cleander yanked the bedroll off his shoulder. The thug's fist lashed out. Cleander ducked, hand scrabbling at the roll of rags in his hands. The thug reached under the layers of his tunic and pulled a length of chain from his waist. Barbs glittered on the edges of the sharpened links. The thug swung. Cleander ducked again, hand reaching inside the bedroll. The weapon hit the floor, and snapped back into the air. Koleg was moving behind the thug. The chain whipped out. Cleander jerked aside. A barb caught his right shoulder and bit deep. The thug yanked, and Cleander lurched forwards, pain rushing through him. Blood spread across his tunic from his shoulder.

Cleander could see Koleg stepping up behind the thug, right hand wreathed with blue lightning. The thug's lips pulled back in a grinning snarl. Rows of hooked metal teeth glinted in his mouth. He yanked the chain again. Cleander went with the force of the pull and slammed his knuckles into the thug's throat. The man staggered, choking. The barb ripped from Cleander's shoulder. Fresh pain burst through him, but his hand had found the grip of the needler hidden inside his bedroll. He pulled the pistol free as the links arced down again.

Blue arcs enveloped the thug's head. His body jerked, muscles spasming, jaws clamping down on his tongue. Blood poured down his chin. Cleander saw Koleg's fingers closed around the base of the man's neck. The polished armatures of the shock-gloves shone as they discharged power.

'You shoot now,' said Koleg.

Cleander brought the pistol up and squeezed the trigger. The gun's hiss was lost under the crackle of electrical discharge. The toxin sliver hit the thug in the right eye and he dropped, muscles still twitching as he hit the floor.

Cleander stepped back, breathing hard. Shadows were moving behind the fabric hangings. Shouts echoed off the cavern ceiling. Koleg dropped to one knee and pulled grenades and weapons from under his coat, laying them on the floor in neat rows.

'That was not optimal,' said the soldier.

'At least we know we found the right place,' replied Cleander.

Cleander ripped open the rest of his bedroll. Objects tumbled out as blood scattered from his wounded arm. He grabbed a falling injector with his good hand and smacked it into his shoulder next to the wound. The cocktail of numb, spur and blood coagulant poured into him an instant after the needle punched through his skin. He let out a sharp breath. Koleg looked up at him, and tossed him a compact filter mask. Cleander caught it and shook the straps free. Koleg already had his mask on, his eyes hidden behind a slot visor set in a white ceramic faceplate. A short chrome cylinder projected from each side of the mask's chin.

'How long until they find us?' asked Cleander.

A shadow loomed next to one of the hangings. A chain blade roared to life, and sliced down through the fabric. Cleander brought the pistol up and put two needles into the shadow. The figure dropped, ripping the hole wide as it fell, chain blade growling in its death grip. Another shape was moving behind it. Cleander could see the shadow of a handgun. He shot again, heard a noise from behind him and spun, putting another shot into a silhouette.

'Secure your mask,' called Koleg, his voice flat and metallic as it came from his own mask's speakers. He held a pistol with a short, tubular barrel. The broken breech of the weapon was wide enough to swallow a shot glass.

Cleander pulled the mask over his head, the rubber seals pressed into his face. The world beyond the photo-visor became a twilight blue. More shadows were moving beyond the screens. He heard the clunk of a gun arming.

'Secure,' he shouted, hearing his own voice echo flat from his speaker.

Koleg nodded, dropped a grenade shell into the pistol launcher, and closed the breech with a flick of his wrist.

Gunfire ripped through the fabric screens. Cleander dropped to the floor as the bullets sawed through the air above him. The torn hangings swayed and his eye caught the flash of muzzle flare. He sent three needles into the space behind the flash, and the gunfire stopped. Koleg, unmoved, aimed the pistol launcher up and pulled the trigger. The grenade thumped into the air, hit the ceiling above and burst in a grey cloud of gas. The spent casing spun to the ground as Koleg cracked the launcher, and dropped another grenade into the breech. He fired again, the shot arcing high over the fabric hangings, then again and again, in a quick, remorseless rhythm.

Grey and cyan fog rolled through the cavern, sinking from the roof, spreading between the cloth hangings. For an instant there was a muffled lull in noise. Then the screaming boiled up, rending the air as terror ripped from a hundred throats. Weeping and shouting blended with the cacophony, as the hallucinogen and terror gas flooded the cavern. Inside his mask, Cleander gulped the sanitised air. It tasted slightly metallic.

Koleg bent down and began to gather up the rest of his equipment, then shrugged into a twin shoulder harness. A macrostubber sat in the left holster, and the pistol grenade launcher went into the empty right holster, the grenades into loops and pouches across his chest. Cleander scooped up his own collection of trinkets. Two heavy rings went onto each hand, a power dagger in a sheath onto his left forearm, and a patch over his left eye socket.

Koleg moved over to the door in the pillar base. The thug's key was still in the lock. Around them the sounds of panic rolled with the spreading fog. Cleander clicked a switch on the side of his mask, and his view through the visor snapped into cold black broken by splashes of red and yellow body heat.

'We proceed?' asked Koleg, drawing his macrostubber pistol from its holster. Cleander moved up next to him, and gripped the key. The lock turned smoothly. Cleander felt the door shudder as bolts thumped back into the frame. He pulled it wide. A flight of stairs spiralled down into the dark. Traces of green warmth moved in the blue-stained cold of Cleander's sight.

'We proceed,' he said and stepped through.

III

Prior Prefectus Gul paused as he crossed the threshold of the western sub-chapel. Candles burned on the altar dominating the far end of the long chamber, filling the nave with the warm glow of flames, but leaving the rest to shadows. The candle in Gul's right hand lit a circle of floor around him, but then slid off into the quiet gloom. Lumn had stopped three paces behind Gul, and waited, head bowed, arms folded in his wide sleeves. His face was wide, the flesh soft beneath his tonsured hair. In the low light the grey of Lumn's robes seemed liked folded shadow.

'Wait for me in the south transept,' said Gul. Lumn bowed his head even lower, then turned and moved away into the darkness of the chapel's main vault. Gul watched him go for a second. Lumn was his Silent Acolyte, an order whose entire existence revolved around serving the spiritual leaders of the Crow Complex. Conditioned to obedience and secrecy, the Silent Acolytes completed their novitiate training by having their tongues cut from their mouths. They were supposed to be utterly trustworthy, and Gul had never had reason to doubt Lumn's devotion. But trust was a coin made of false gold.

Gul stepped into the sub-chapel, and let the quiet of night gather around him. Like the rest of the High Chapel, it was almost deserted. During the day, Dominicus' sun would rise through the sky, and its light would fall through the chapel's windows and crystal dome, illuminating the faithful. Once the sun began to fall, the prayers faded and those who had been granted a place at twilight prayer left the chapel to sleep in silence. Only the members of the order of the Eternal Light moved amongst the pews and pillars, tending the candles that burned in the one hundred and eight shrines. As the second most senior brother in all the orders of the Crow Complex, Gul was one of the only other souls who saw the High Chapel in the dark.

He liked the night. It was a sea of calm in the constant whirl that was the governance of the monastery complex. That you could only hear yourself think when this supposed place of peace was empty, was an irony that struck him every time he stepped into the High Chapel. Not that he ever thought of it as a place of true peace, nor of the blessings that were given within its walls as anything but empty lies. The Imperial Creed was a doctrine of blood and greed, and bloated power feeding on the fear of the faithful. The Emperor did not protect, and never had. He was a man who did extraordinary things, who had earned the Imperium he had created, but a man none the less. For all his power, one might as well take a hook and line to the sea and fish for truth as pray to the Emperor for deliverance, enlightenment or mercy.

Gul had not always known that the Emperor was not divine. Once he had been like all the other credulous fools. Now he held the truth locked inside his skull, hidden by competence and masked by piety. He could smile at a grossly fat prelate exhorting starving pilgrims to beware the lure of gluttony. He could watch the preachers dole out blessings while the devotional servitors followed them to collect coin from the grateful. He could do these things because he knew the truth. That core of secrets locked inside him gave him a strength that the Imperial Creed never had. He was a heretic, and he was blessed to be so.

He stepped towards the sub-chapel's altar, glancing at the candle that marked the time. His rendezvous with his contact in the Tenth Path was not until the next division, but he liked to arrive first. It gave him comfort, a veneer of control over what was happening. Besides, it gave him time to think. His footsteps echoed softly under the gaze of the stone saints lining the walls. It had been sixty days since his last meeting, and he had not expected to be summoned again so soon. Had something changed? What would be asked of him? Was there something wrong?

He was a pace from the altar when the candle flames rippled. A breath of cold air touched the back of his neck. He whirled around, eyes going to the arch he had entered through.

There was nothing there, just the distant light of torches falling in the main transept. Cold air gusted past him again, and the candles on the altar guttered. Somewhere a door banged shut. The air was still again, the dark in the sub-chapel almost total now. Footsteps echoed behind him, and Gul turned.

'Who is there?' he called, and the stone echoed back his voice in fading whispers.

'...is there?'

'Who...'

'... there... there... there...?'

The afterglow of the extinguished candle flames clung to his retinas as he turned and stared at the dark.

'Prior Prefectus Aristas Gul,' said a voice from behind him. He whirled back, eyes wide, mouth dry.

Fire sparked in front of him. Gul flinched, but the flame held steady, a single tongue of orange in the black. The image of a hand holding a burning taper formed next to the light, and then the flaring light caught the outline of a hooded figure. Black and white checks ran around the sleeves of the red robes.

'You should not be here,' snapped Gul, his voice ringing high. He could feel cold snaking down his skin. 'I demand–'

'A scholar once told me that humans lit candles in prayer before they even knew they were not alone in the cosmos,' said the robed figure. The hand holding the taper reached out, and put the flame to the wick of a candle. The fire caught. 'Before they knew that their gods were lies, they still drew hope from that one small act.'

Gul felt his mouth open to call out, but the words caught before they could reach his tongue. The robed figure turned. The bronze hand hanging on the robed man's chest glinted. Gul's frozen mind finally registered the colours and details of the figure's robes. He could see the hilt of a sword and the butt of a gun projecting up behind the man's hood.

'You are not Abbot Crayling,' he said, anger overcoming fear. 'You are not of the Order of Castigation. Who are you?'

A swish of fabric jerked Gul's eyes to the arched doorway at the other end of the chapel. A slender figure in red robes stood outlined against the glow from beyond. Her hood was down, and he could see the ruddy 'X' crossing her face beneath a shaved scalp. A heavy step rang behind him and a hunched figure appeared from the dark, muscles and fat rippling under crimson fabric as the man hefted a double-handed hammer.

His skin felt tight, his blood a racing beat of ice in his flesh. Fears and possibilities formed and spun in his mind: discovery, betrayal, escape. He should run. He should make for the small door behind the altar and flee. He should call out. Lumn might still be close enough to hear him. But he did not move or speak. Instead his mouth repeated the last words they had spoken.

'Who are you?' he breathed.

The tall man with the sword across his back reached up and lowered his hood. The face beneath was young and strong, long black hair pulled back in a topknot above hard, dark eyes.

'I am Covenant,' said the man, 'and I am here to offer you a chance of absolution.'

IV

Cold darkness swallowed Cleander as he descended the spiral stairs. The world was painted in blue in his infra-visor. Only he and Koleg stood out, their shapes yellow and red with warmth. They had closed the door into the sleeping cavern, and had been descending for long enough that they had left all light far behind. After a while he had switched to dark vision, but there were no scraps of light for it to gather, just a grey blur at the edge of sight. He had switched back to the blindness of infra-vision, and moved by touch, left hand running over the rough stone of the wall.

'These catacombs run deep,' he muttered after a while.

'A fact that we knew at mission briefing,' said Koleg.

Cleander shivered, suddenly wishing that he had something more substantial than pilgrim rags to keep him warm. 'It should not be this cold – there are no air currents, no running water. So why is it getting colder?' he said. Koleg hesitated behind him. He turned, and looked at the soldier. Koleg's shape was a bright rainbow of body heat.

'The temperature is stable,' said Koleg. 'It isn't getting colder.'

Cleander felt himself become very still. Ice ran over his skin. In his eyes the colours of the infra-sight swam, switching and blurring. His teeth rattled against each other in his mouth. He turned back to the darkness beneath the next step. He reached out for the wall. His fingers slid into empty air. He flinched, but kept his hand extended. The cold bit into his bare skin. He moved his hand to the side, breathing slowly. His fingers touched stone. It felt warm, as though it had been warmed by the sun.

'There is a door on my right,' he said, carefully. 'Follow the direction of my right arm.'

Koleg moved close, hand macrostubber levelled, one hand on Cleander's shoulder.

'Ready,' said Koleg.

Cleander's right hand flexed on the grip of his needler.

'Moving,' he said, and stepped into the waiting emptiness beyond the door.

A deeper chill washed over him, as though he had stepped through a cascade of water. The view in his infra-visor flashed, bubbles of yellow and red heat popping against blue. He snapped the visor to normal vision. For a moment the black remained pressed against his eyes. Then light began to sketch a reality around him. A blue-green glow spread up columns framing eight openings set to either side of a long chamber.

The columns supporting the arches were carved from a stone that glistened like glass. A long pool of liquid ran down the centre of the floor, its surface a black mirror. Cleander stepped forwards, and Koleg moved past him, pistol levelled, tracking between each of the archways.

'This is it,' said Cleander. 'This is where they were bringing us.'

'This is the target?'

Cleander did not respond. His eyes flicked over the chamber. For a second he thought had seen something sinuous move under the stone surface of the wall, as though it were a sheet of glass opening on an ocean.

'Who was it that the big lug said he was bringing us to see?' said Cleander, softly. He was suddenly wishing that he had argued for a different approach in tackling the Tenth Path, an approach that included a platoon of his household mercenaries. Or a Space Marine strike team.

'The confessor...' said Koleg.

Cleander turned to answer, and stopped. A tall, hunched statue stood under a white shroud at the far end of the chamber. The fabric stirred as though in a breeze. The scent of crushed flowers and spoiled meat brushed Cleander's senses. Rage bubbled up inside him, staining his thoughts red. Whispers chirped at the edges of his mind, promising things he never knew he wanted. He shut out the thoughts and sensations.

He knew what this was; the warp was close, shivering just beyond the skin of reality, feeling for a crack through which to pour. To others, even that touch would be enough to force them to their knees, eyes wide but seeing nothing. Cleander had touched the warp and seen its true face many times, and though he knew better than to think himself immune to its promises, he also knew himself well enough to see those promises as empty. He was not a good man, he was very far from a good man. He knew the power of wealth and lies, and enjoyed using both. He cared for few, and saw most people as expendable and worthless at best. He had no ideals, and his few beliefs all had a price. These were facts that he had never denied, but they were not weakness; they were armour against false desire.

Koleg swayed where he stood, and then moved forwards, gun raised. Cleander stepped to follow, and then paused. He glanced up, and then back to the pool of water running down the centre of the room. The ceiling above was vaulted stone. Perhaps it had been the crypt of one of the first temples raised on Dominicus Prime, now buried deep beneath the mountain of stone that was the Crow Complex. Handprints covered the ceiling, hundreds of handprints in dried, dark liquid. Cleander paused.

'Koleg,' he said, carefully.

'Yes?'

'The pool,' said Cleander. Koleg snapped a glance at it, and then back to the space beyond his gun.

'I see it,' said Koleg.

Cleander stepped forwards, kneeling slowly. He stared at the black gloss surface. The water beneath was black, and Cleander could not tell if that was because he could not see through it, or if it was perfectly clear and he was looking down into an abyss.

'It reflects nothing,' he said, and reached out to touch it.

'What are you doing?' called Koleg.

'The confessor,' he said. 'That is what is supposed to be down here. The first steps of damnation are always wrapped in the costume of piety – isn't that what Josef keeps on saying? So when all those lost souls come down here, they come to confess. And why do the pious confess?' His fingers were just above the surface. 'To be washed clean.'

He touched the water.

Circles spread across the pool, struck the sides and rebounded. Water lapped over the edges.

'Is this wise?' said Koleg as he moved next to Cleander.

'No,' said Cleander, and the word was a puff of white in the suddenly freezing air. 'But if I was wise I would not be here in the first place.'

More water was splashing out of the pool as its surface began to chop and heave. A low moan ran around the chamber, and Cleander looked up for a second. When he looked back, it was into a face floating beneath the surface of the water. He leapt to his feet. Koleg spun.

The face was pale, the flesh fat under blue-veined skin. Silver hair swirled around it, billowing in the water. Its mouth was open, tongue pink between white teeth. The eyes were closed as though in sleep, or peaceful death. Cleander tried to move, to bring his needler up, but he was frozen in place, eyes locked on the image forming beneath the waves. A torso appeared beneath the face, then arms and legs. Lines of stitched scars criss-crossed flesh. Silver tubes ran into the tips of its fingers and ran off into the depths. Cleander's heart was a paused beat in his chest. The face in the water opened its eyes. He had an impression of colour swirling around ragged pupils. Ice was spreading across the floor from the pool edge.

+Help,+ said a voice that echoed in Cleander's skull. +Help me.+

He felt his limbs moving, felt himself bend down to the water, reaching beneath to pull the figure out into the air.

+Free me.+

'Von Castellan!' shouted Koleg, close but so far away. 'Stand back, now!'

+Please,+ whispered the voice in his head.

A hand gripped Cleander's arm and yanked him back. He swore, surged up, confusion and anger roaring through him. Koleg shoved him away, and Cleander's eyes cleared.

Figures stepped from the black spaces of the archways. Tatters of soaking cloth hung from them. Jagged circle tattoos slid over the exposed skin of their arms and necks. Darkness shone from the marks, shredding light, fuming night. Grey ash powdered their faces. Their eyes were closed, and frost breathed from their lips. Serrated knives and barbed chains hung from their hands.

Koleg fired. A tongue of flame ripped from the macrostubber. The shroud covering the shape at the end of the chamber billowed, and the lost pilgrims, who had found their way along the Tenth Path to a revelation that they could no longer escape, leapt forwards in a blur of sharp edges.

V

'What are you talking about?' said Gul, his eyes wide as he stared at Covenant. He could feel calm draining from him. 'This is a gross violation of–'

'The Tenth Path,' said Covenant softly.

Gul breathed out, mind racing through what was happening.

Covenant turned back to the altar, reached out, and lit a second candle from the first.

'Three years ago someone came to you and asked you to help him keep a secret,' said Covenant. 'He said to you that he saw a connection between you both, a shared vision of the truth. You were scared. You wondered how someone could know thoughts you had never spoken to another soul.'

Gul felt his hands start to tremble.

'Are you...' he said. 'Are you with him?'

'He said that you were right, that the faith you had turned

from was false, that there was nothing divine in the universe beside what we made, that to believe otherwise was to create your own prison. He said that everything you had been told was a lie.' Covenant's eyes stayed fixed on the twin candle flames. 'And then he asked you to serve, to help others who saw the truth, to protect them, and give them aid and shelter. And that is what you have done, prior. You have found ways of hiding people, of diverting funds, and deflecting attention from a cult that you have never seen.'

Shock shuddered through Gul. His head was spinning. Anger flared up, hot and bright.

'You don't know what you are talking about,' he snarled. 'You really have no idea what you are—'

'The Inquisition,' said Covenant. 'The man who came to you said that he was of the Inquisition.' He raised his hand, and opened his fingers. Luminous lines spread across the palm as an electoo lit.

Gul stared at the glowing image of a stylised 'I' broken by three bars across its middle. It was a sigil he had only seen once before, and then, as now, its implication stole every thought from his skull.

'And the Inquisition is something that I know very well,' said Covenant.

'But he *was* of the Inquisition,' Gul heard himself say.

Covenant gave a single slow nod.

'Yes.'

'Why did he... need me?'

'Because he needed someone to protect the seed he planted here until he could harvest its flower.'

'I don't understand,' said Gul. 'He was an inquisitor, and he said that I served humanity. Yet if you are an inquisitor how can you condemn me for doing his work?'

'Because everything you have believed is a lie. The Tenth Path are not lost souls that share your misguided heresy. They are a coven devoted to darkness and ruin. What you have sheltered and protected is a cradle of monsters.'

'I don't believe you...'

'Yes, you do,' said Covenant.

Gul felt the shaking start at his feet, and roll up through muscle and skin. Something in him wanted to shout that he was innocent, that it was just another layer of lies. But something in Covenant's voice cut through that tissue of comfort. He felt his knees begin to fold.

A strong hand caught his shoulder and steadied him. Gul glanced behind him and saw a scarred face in the shadow of a hood, and realised that the fat man with the hammer had stepped behind him without a noise.

'Steady,' growled the man softly. 'Remember what you were, prior. Face this with courage.'

Gul blinked, confused, but felt his back straighten and some strength return to his limbs. Covenant remained still, gaze fixed, face expressionless. Gul felt moisture on his cheek, and raised his hand to touch his face.

I am crying, he realised. 'What...' he stammered. 'What can I do?'

'Before dawn comes the Tenth Path will be no more. There is nothing more you can do to aid or condemn them. But the one who began this, the one who deceived you, he lives, and above all else he fears what you can give me.'

'I will tell you everything,' said Gul.

A breath of cold air stirred his robes, and prickled his skin. 'I...' he began to say, but Covenant's head had jerked up, eyes moving across the shadows beyond the altar.

'How many ways in are there?' growled the fat man behind Gul.

29

'What?' stammered Gul. 'The main arch, the priest's door, and–' the words caught in his throat as he realised what the draught of air meant. 'And... and the way through the undercroft.'

'Severita,' called Covenant.

'I feel it, lord,' came a woman's voice from close by the arch into the main chapel. 'Something is here.'

'What is happening?' hissed Gul.

'A watcher,' said Covenant. 'The man who you served would have sent a servant to watch over you, to make sure you did not stray.' The breath of cold air was stronger now. The candle flames rippled.

'Where is the entrance to the undercroft?' said Covenant.

'Here,' said Gul, taking a step forwards without thinking. A warm glow had filled him suddenly. 'It's just behind this part of the altar. There is a trick to it,' he said, and felt a smile form on his face as he spoke. 'A trick lock that releases a panel. I have often wondered why anyone would conceal such a thing. As an amusement, perhaps.' He laughed. His mind was clear. There was nothing to fear. Everything was simple. He just needed to show them where the hidden door was. He heard the one called Covenant shout something, but the words were distant, soft, meaningless. All that mattered was the next step he needed to take.

A thin figure stood before him in the shadows. Pale robes hung from it, a hood hiding its bowed head. Recognition sparked in the fog of Gul's thoughts.

'Lumn?' he said, and felt the warm dullness of his thoughts shift as he frowned at his Silent Acolyte. 'What are you doing here, boy? I said to wait in the south transept.'

Lumn did not answer, but raised his head. The face beneath the hood was Lumn's but its eyes were holes, and for an instant

Gul could not see the chapel, just the dark and stars swirling against the blood- and violet-stained sheet of night.

Then something lifted him from his feet and spun him over, as gunfire tore through the air.

VI

Cleander brought the needler up and squeezed the trigger twice. Toxin splinters hissed into the nearest pilgrim's throat. The man crumpled, the chain in his fist whipping out with the last of his momentum. Cleander ducked. The chain whistled over his head. Another pilgrim was on him before he could stand. A knife sliced across his forearm. He flinched back, and shot the pilgrim in the face.

'Koleg!' he shouted.

More figures were coming from the arches on either side of the chamber. Two ran at Cleander. Neither had hands. Hooked blades projected from the stumps of their wrists. The first swung at him. He ducked under the blow, came up and levelled his closed fist. The digi-weapons in his rings fired. A stream of plasma hit the hook-armed figure, and blasted him into a cloud of ash and screaming heat. Another man came at him, hook arm arcing down towards his head. Cleander stamped his foot out, felt bone break under his heel, and the pilgrim was falling backwards. He rammed the muzzle of his needler into the man's face and squeezed the trigger three times.

Cleander raised his head, breathing hard. A mass of figures was pouring from the arches, eyes closed, weapons reaching.

'Koleg!'

'Down!' shouted Koleg.

Cleander dropped.

Koleg's macrostubber purred thunder. The first rank of pilgrims fell, torsos almost cut in two by the deluge of rounds. Koleg panned the pistol left, scything into the crowd of bodies. Blood puffed into the air, scattering across the black surface of the mirror pool. The macrostubber clicked dry.

More pilgrims were scrabbling over the bodies of the dead, teeth bared, eyes twitching beneath closed eyelids. Cleander stood as Koleg levelled his pistol launcher and fired. Fire burst across the far side of the chamber. The visor in Cleander's mask blinked to near black. Gasping cries rolled with the roar of the inferno. Limbs thrashed in the blaze. As his visor switched to mundane sight, he could see mouths moving in snarling faces as the flesh cooked from skulls.

Cleander moved forwards, needle pistol in both hands. Koleg was snapping a drum into his macrostubber. The surface of the pool was a mirror of flames. The fire coiled in the air, tongues spiralling together, roaring with the screams of the dying. The grey shroud covering the statue at the end of the chamber caught light, and dissolved in a curtain of ashes. The thing – that was not a statue – stood tall and shook itself free of cinders.

It had started as a human, or perhaps many humans. It looked like a man, but a man so tall that its shoulders touched the ceiling. Its skin was the white of marble. Rows of red eyes ran down its cheeks. Muscles bunched as it moved, and blood seeped from the iron bolts hammered into flesh. Chains circled its limbs and the links rang as it stepped forwards. Cleander knew what it was, though he wished with all his heart that he did not. It was a host to the powers of the warp, a conduit to the hungering beyond. It was a creature of Chaos.

The air in the chamber reeked of sulphur. The creature took a juddering step forwards. Koleg fired. The creature raised a hand. Cleander had an impression of long fingers and sharpness. Time stuttered, and the bullets melted in the air. Sparks and metal droplets scattered onto the surface of the pool. Koleg dropped the macrostubber, his hands a blur as he reached for the grenade launcher. The creature roared. A spear of fire ripped from between its teeth. Koleg dived aside as fire washed where he had stood. The creature dropped to all fours, and leapt through the blaze.

+Help me...+

Cleander heard the voice in the back of his head. He took the last step towards the ice-crusted pool, and looked down. The figure was still there, just beneath the surface. Ghost light blazed in its eyes. Its hands were moving, paddling weakly, tugging against the silver tubes linked to its fingers. He could see its lips moving, could see teeth glinting like pearls beside the wound where its tongue had been.

On the other side of the chamber, Koleg was rolling over, the right side of his body on fire. The creature from beneath the shroud stretched back to its full height. The air shimmered around it. Cleander could feel heat radiating from it. The figure in the pool was writhing under the ice, and he could see an echo of the warp creature's movements in the desperate thrashing. They were connected, the host creature and the body tethered in the pool. He should do something now that he understood that fact, he should...

+Help...+

Sensations were spinning through Cleander's skull. He felt his gun drop from his fingers. Everything was a rolling cloud of competing voices from his memory: his father shouting at him, the leaden disappointment in his sister's eyes, the stillness of Covenant.

+Help–+

He punched his hands through the water's surface. Ice cracked. Wet warmth surrounded his arms, soft and thick, like blood. He touched flesh, gripped, and twisted, and he felt something snap. Time blinked.

And then he was falling forwards into the dark embrace of the water.

VII

Gul hit the floor. Air thumped from his lungs. He rolled over and gasped. There was a slow quality to everything, as though his mind were a jammed chronometer catching up with time. He was on the floor next to the tier of pews that ran down the right of the chapel. The atmosphere was bright with explosions. The place where he had been standing in front of the altar was ten paces away. Something had picked him up and flipped him through the air like a hand batting away a toy. Lumn stood in the dark beyond the altar. Except it was not Lumn.

The young man's face was a mask broken by black holes where his mouth and eyes had been. Colour and shape distorted around him, light casting shadow, shadow burning with light. Bolt rounds burst in mid-air around him. Shrapnel tore the wood of the seating. Splinters spun out. Lumn turned his head towards Gul, and stepped forwards. Covenant stepped across his path. Light haloed the inquisitor, and the air in front of him shimmered. A wall of invisible force blasted from Covenant. Broken pews tore from the floor. Lumn met the wall of force with a raised hand. Light shattered just beyond his palm. A shockwave rolled outwards. Gul felt his ears pop.

To his left he could see the woman with the marked face vault onto the pews, fire blazing from her bolt pistols. One of the bolts stuck Lumn in the shoulder and punched him off his feet in a spray of shrapnel and blood. Covenant was moving, the great sword sliding from his shoulder in a single blur of sharpness and activating a power field. Lumn hit the floor, and the sword descended above him. He vanished. Covenant's sword struck the floor. Stone sheared into shards.

A shadow rose above Gul. He looked up. Lumn stood on the tier above him. Black smoke coiled from where the bolt round had ripped away his shoulder and half of his face. Worms of pale light burrowed through the bloody flesh, and Gul realised that muscle and bone were bubbling up to fill the wound. The edges of Lumn's form were like a ragged cloak blowing in the wind. The pews crumbled to glowing ash around him. He pointed at Gul and his hands seemed to grow, spreading through the air like the shadows reaching from flame. Pain exploded in Gul's chest. Ice formed on his lips as he screamed.

The fat man with the hammer charged from behind Gul, muscle surging under fat as he spun his warhammer. Lumn raised his hands, and to Gul they seemed to be claws of hooked bone. The man swung the hammer, roaring, face locked in rage. Claws and hammerhead met, and suddenly Lumn was going backwards, shadows coiling around him, and there was blood mixing with the embers.

Bolt rounds exploded against the shadows around Lumn. Gul could see the woman with the bolt pistols leaping across the chapel. He heard words lift into the air between the roar of her guns. 'Blessed father of mankind...' the voice rose high and clear, echoing from the high roof. 'May my hands be your talons...' Fire blistered the gloom.

The man with the hammer glanced over his shoulder.

'Get up! Move!' he shouted at Gul, as Lumn stepped from the fire of the explosions, and punched his clawed hand into the man's side. The man gasped, eyes wide, blood on his lips. Lumn lifted him from the floor.

'For I am your Seraph...' The woman leapt across the last yards between her and Lumn, pistols still firing.

Lumn's head turned towards her. His face was a mass of red flesh, his eyes holes in a bloody skull. Lightning and blue fire lit the dark, and the woman was crumpling to the floor, the words of her prayer lost on her lips. Lumn threw the man with the hammer across the chapel, and stepped forwards, his form flickering like the frames of a faulty pict feed. He no longer looked like the young man who had walked at Gul's side for three years. He no longer looked even human. His body pulsed with wet sinew and cold fire as he reached out for Gul. The clawed fingers closed over Gul's mouth. Sharp claw tips bit into his cheeks as Lumn pulled him off the floor like a child lifting a broken toy.

+Silence,+ hissed a voice in Gul's thoughts as he saw blackness fold around him.

The sword blow severed Lumn's arm at the elbow. White light flooded Gul's eyes as the power field flared. A cry filled the air, rising higher and higher. Half blind, Gul had time to see Lumn reel back, blood pouring from the stump of his arm. Covenant followed him, turning with the weight of his sword as he cut. Lightning flashed, and Lumn, or whatever had called itself Lumn, was falling, its blood burning as it scattered through the air.

VIII

The memory came to Cleander as he drowned.

'How many choices do I have?' he had asked.

Covenant had held Cleander's gaze for a second, dark eyes unblinking.

'There is always a choice.'

'Information or execution?'

Covenant shook his head.

'Execution is kindness in this universe, Duke Von Castellan, and you know nothing that I want to know.'

'So?' Cleander had said, raising his eyebrow. 'That is supposed to be your threat? You should work on your technique.'

'You are not a coward, and you are not unintelligent, so please do not insult my intelligence by saying that you don't understand what I am saying.'

'Obliteration...' Cleander had said at last.

'For you,' said Covenant, 'and for your family, and everyone you ever knew and cared for. Those that are not found will be hunted for all time without hope of forgiveness.'

'You can't do that. No one can do that.'

'I can, and you know that I can,' said Covenant.

'If I am the man you say I am, then you should know that I don't care about anyone else.'

'But you do.'

Cleander had not replied for a long moment, and then nodded once at the inquisitor.

'What is the other choice?'

Hands gripped his back and hauled him out of the dark. He broke the surface of the water, gasped for air, and vomited. Water and bile poured from his mouth as he coughed and heaved air into his lungs.

'You are alive,' said Koleg from above him.

'Your...' Cleander vomited again. 'Your observations are as insightful as ever.'

'It was intended to reassure you.'

'Good...' gasped Cleander. The world in front of his eyes was smeared with grey and pain. 'Good...'

He rolled over and tried to sit up. The chamber was quiet. Flames still crawled over the heaped corpses, and a layer of smoke was gathering beneath the roof and flowing through the archways into the spaces beyond. The pool of water stirred with the waves from Cleander's exit, but it was just water, its surface reflecting the devastation in rippled fragments. A corpse floated close to the edge of the pool, its head waving on its broken neck.

'Where is the... monster?' he asked.

'The host creature fell when you broke the neck of the thing in the pool,' said Koleg. He pointed at the far side of the pool where a heap of skin lay on the wet stone like a discarded coat.

Koleg shifted his weight, and Cleander noticed that the soldier was holding his right arm against his body. His scorched mask and visor hung around his neck, and glossy burns marked the side of his face. Not for the first time, Cleander wondered if the alterations made to Koleg's brain removed pain or just the man's ability to feel the emotion of being in pain. He felt his own hands begin to tremble.

'It was as Covenant expected,' said Koleg, nodding at the floating corpse in the pool. 'Another warp conduit and symbiotic possession, just like on Agresis.'

'Yes, yes... just like it,' said Cleander, not really listening. His limbs felt numb and his head was swimming. 'Help me up.' Koleg reached down with his good arm. Cleander gripped the arm and pulled himself up with a stream of swearing. He swayed on his feet, looked around the floor, frowning. 'Where is my gun?' Koleg held it up. Cleander nodded, took it, and began to limp towards the arch that led to the stairs.

'Where are you going?' called Koleg. 'This area will need to be cleansed.'

'Someone else's problem, someone else's job. I am going

to somewhere where the transmitter will be able to reach our lord and master, and then...' he trailed off, pausing, blinking. He thought of the reflection he had glimpsed in the surface of the pool before he had touched its surface: a man with dark hair and beard, his skin marked by time and scarred by blades, one eye a pit, the other a flicker of black under his own gaze. 'Then I am going to drink more than is necessary, and then, I guess, I am going to wait to hear where I will next serve my penance.'

He limped on to the arch, before turning and looking back. Koleg stood where he had been before, face unreadable in the light of the cooling fire.

'Are you coming?' asked Cleander. After a second Koleg gave a nod and followed him.

IX

Gul turned his head, blinking at the sunlight. Blue sky curved in a dome above him. The chair beneath him was carved from driftwood. Slabs of smooth stone ran away from him until they met the sea. Waves lapped against the stone edge, sending spray into the air to cool the warm breeze. Beyond that, the sea was a wide band of deeper blue beneath the sky. He knew where he was, knew that if he looked behind him he would see the tower of Solar Truth rising from the land like a shard of broken glass. He also did not know how he could be there. It had been three decades since he had last been in this place, since he had left his home to follow his faith. He turned to look behind him.

'This is very pleasant,' said a voice in front of him.

His head snapped around. A woman sat in front of him. At a glance she looked young. Red hair rose in the wind around a slim face. Her eyes were dark, her mouth tilted in a smirk. A silver carafe and two crystal goblets of amber wine sat on a stone table between them. He noticed that the goblet nearest the woman was almost empty, as though she had been drinking from it for a while. The green silk of her robe shimmered in the sunlight as she picked up the goblet and brought it to her lips.

'Try it,' she said. 'It is worth it.'

Gul frowned. Memories of the chapel on Dominicus Prime pushed into his thoughts, the flash of gunfire, and the sound of screams rose, but they seemed distant, unconnected to him and unimportant.

He picked up the goblet and took a sip.

'Where did you get this?' he breathed. 'They never let this vintage out of the arch-prior's personal cellar.'

'Oh, we have the means to get almost anything we like,' said the woman. 'But in this case I got it from you, Aristas.' He looked up at the sound of his first name. The woman smiled, and gestured at the sea and sky around them. 'Just like I got all of this from you.'

Gul stared at her.

'Who–?'

'You can call me Mylasa,' she said before he could finish the question. 'Do you like it? It was one of the few places in your head that you remember with happiness. Seemed like a good place for you to have this moment. Shame it could not be longer, really.'

'What?'

'I – or should I say *we*, because what is life but not being able to do anything without it being at someone else's bidding – have just searched your mind, prior. I have stripped down all of the memories I could find, and where I needed your help, I have inflicted pain and nightmares on you until you told me – there I go again, of course I mean us – until you told *us* everything we needed to know.'

Memories came into focus in his head.

'Covenant...' he breathed. 'You are with the inquisitor.'

'Yes,' she nodded, and took a sip of her wine. 'And before you ask, the pain and the screaming are over. We are done. *You* are done. I removed the memories of what I did. This is a... oh, I don't know... a gift, a kindness to ease my torturer's soul.' Mylasa put her goblet down on the table, filled it again, and took a gulp, then sighed.

'If you have inflicted pain on me, but I cannot remember it, then what is to be my true punishment?'

'You are a heretic, prior, but you are not an evil man. There is actually a difference, but don't tell anyone. You are just a fool and very unlucky.' She looked over her shoulder at the waves rolling across the sea.

'So the chapel, Lumn, Covenant, it all happened?'

'Some time ago, in fact,' said Mylasa. 'It took a while to make sure that we had every detail of what you knew.'

'The Tenth Path...' he said. 'I had no idea. I don't even...'

'I know,' she said. 'But innocence proves nothing, as some-one very perceptive once pointed out. You were used, prior, and so you suffer.'

'By the man who came to me before,' he said, 'by the man who claimed to be an inquisitor.'

'Oh, he was an inquisitor,' she said, and he noticed that the smirk had gone from her lips. 'Inquisitor Goldoran Talicto, in fact – Scion of Gorgonate Collegium, Scourge of the Nine Stars of Nix.'

'But...'

'There are truths in the universe, prior, truths so big that to know them is death or madness. The first truth is that

every whisper of daemons that thirst for souls and torment –
those whispers are just a shadow of the greater truth. There are
creatures that wish to enslave mankind, creatures so powerful
that it is easiest to call them gods and their avatars, daemons.
To know this truth is to be condemned to death, prior.'

Gul felt cold prickle his skin despite the warmth of the sun.

'How can that be true?'

Mylasa continued as though she had not heard his question.
'The second great truth is that those who are meant to protect
us from such forces are divided as much as they are united.
And sometimes – once upon a blessed rare age – one of them
falls to something worse than divergent opinion. They become
a slave to their own view of mankind's salvation.'

'And Inquisitor Talicto is one such–'

'He used you to protect one of his projects. The Tenth Path
were sheltering and nurturing a psyker that they had bonded
to a host that acted as a conduit for the... things from the warp.
It was crude, and luckily was largely a failure.'

'I didn't know,' he said.

'We know, and we know everything that you did to protect
the Tenth Path. Those details will help us to condemn Talicto
in the sight of his peers.' She raised her goblet as though in a
toast. 'You have served the Emperor well.'

'Is that why you are talking to me?' he asked. 'As thanks
from Covenant?'

She laughed, covering her mouth as though choking on her
wine.

'No, I am doing this myself. Covenant would tell you none
of this.'

'But why tell me anything?' he asked.

'Because if you know secrets, sometimes it is good to tell
someone who will never be able to break your trust.'

Gul frowned. He was feeling dizzy. The sun was warm on his skin. He could smell the salt spray from the sea.

'And what is this? A dream? An illusion?'

Mylasa looked at him for a long moment, and then stood, turning away to face the sea.

'Drink the wine,' she said. 'It is really very good.'

X

+It is done,+ said Mylasa. Cleander flinched at the sound of the psyker's thought-voice. He would really rather have not been there, but Covenant had insisted that they all gather in the cell where they had been keeping Prior Prefectus Gul in the weeks since Dominicus Prime.

Cleander glanced at his sister on the other side of the room, but Viola was looking at Covenant, her face emotionless beneath the plaited ivory of her hair. Covenant himself stood at the foot of the slab, robed in grey. Josef stood next to him, the preacher's face mottled with fading bruises, a servitor hovering above his shoulder, gently pulsing blood into his neck through transparent tubes. That Josef was alive at all was a miracle, but perhaps that was the benefit of piety. Koleg leant against the wall to the side, posture and face utterly unreadable. Severita knelt to the side of the prior, the hilt of her sword clasped between her hands, head bowed. The low sound of the ship's engines rumbled through the quiet. They were all waiting, he realised.

'He's dead?' asked Josef, eyes on the body of the prior shackled to the steel slab.

+Yes,+ replied Mylasa. Cleander looked at her reflexively, and then turned away, with a wince. Metal encircled the psyker's neck and head. Bulbous tubes hissed steam into the air, and bundles of wires snaked between blisters of chrome. Her face sat in the mass of machinery like a strangled pearl. Withered limbs hung from the machinery like the mane of a jellyfish, hovering just above the ground. Static crackled around her in oily flashes.

'One less for the edge of your sword, Severita,' said Cleander, hearing the hollow sneer in his voice. The penitent sister did not bother to look up from her prayers. 'Was he expecting another form of forgiveness, I wonder?'

+He died without pain, and with a memory of kinder times,+ said Mylasa. +In this age that is absolution enough.+

'Something for us all to aspire to,' snorted Cleander.

'We have what we need,' said Covenant. Every eye in the chamber moved to him. He was still looking at the body of the prior. 'A conclave of war has been called on Ero. Talicto will be there. And there will be a reckoning.' He looked up, eyes moving slowly over each of them around the slab, and then turned and walked away. The others followed after a second. Cleander lingered, looking down at the dead heretic.

'A kindness...' he muttered, and snorted. 'I think I would rather take the cruelty of life.' He shifted the eyepatch over his empty socket and walked away, leaving the dead to silence.

WARHAMMER
40,000

A Trick of the Light

Josh Reynolds

Lukas was tired.

Exhaustion had become the sum totality of his existence. Fatigue-poisons pumped through his system, slowing everything to a glacial pace. More than once, he stumbled, nearly losing his footing on the ice. The palms of his hands and the soles of his feet were raw and bleeding, where they were not numb.

Everything hurt.

Not just from the cold and the effort. The ache he felt went deeper than that, into the very marrow of him. His gut churned, as if something sought release. A gout of breath escaped his lips, and a groan. A laugh pursued the groan. The laugh circled like a scavenger bird, before dissolving into agonised chuckles.

Everything hurt.

Lukas looked at his hands, to make sure that they were still his. They were bigger than he remembered, thicker. Patches of red – some of it hair, not blood – marked his bare arms. He curled his fingers into fists, and his knuckles popped like shifting ice. Something inside him shifted, changing position, growing larger. Nausea ripsawed through him.

Josh Reynolds

He stumbled and sank to one knee, head bowed against the wind sweeping down from the north. The cold thrummed through him, teasing every nerve. His skin was thicker now, but the cold was as sharp as a serpent's fang. He could see farther, but his eyelids were crusted with ice. His lungs were bigger, but they were filled with the cold. Nonetheless, a fire burned in him.

They called it the Canis Helix, those priests in the great mountain. But he knew it was the blood of the gods. A red, wet wolf, let loose inside him, hollowing him out and filling his empty skin with its strength. A spasm of pain rippled through him, as his spine realigned.

'Click, crack, pop,' he grunted, mimicking the sound of shifting bones. His jaw sagged and something that was as much a moan as a laugh slipped out, to dart from rock to rock until it was swallowed by the vast, white emptiness which surrounded him.

The wilderness into which he had been abandoned was a labyrinth of ice and occasional spurs of stone, of flurrying snow and arctic mist and freezing temperatures. The thick packed ice shifted underfoot, cracking and reforming. High above, great trees clustered against the jagged fangs of rock, marking the border between sky and earth. Past this border, the great peaks of Asaheim. And at their heart, the Fang – the greatest of them all, stretching upwards into the eternal night-sea where the stars floated, like a dagger driven up into the belly of the sky.

'Or maybe it's just drool dripping down from the Star-Wolf's muzzle,' he muttered. His fingers ached. He looked down. 'Ha,' he said, wonderingly. Curved splinters of bone had pushed through his fingertips. Those were new. He laughed and then winced, clutching himself with his new claws.

It hurt to laugh. Lukas did it anyway, forcing the sound out.

46

Laughter was a weapon. His only weapon. The ice, the cold, the gods and their priests, even his own people at times, all wanted him dead. He'd nearly died on the day of his birth, when he'd been cut from his mother's belly, blue-faced and silent. His father had almost cast him to the waves then, but even dying, his mother had been as fierce a she-wolf as ever trod the deck of a raiding ship. And so little Lukas had survived. Had grown, and learned the truth of life, from a broken father and a dead mother, and a tribe which gave little thought to either.

And so, he laughed. The wind howled, and he laughed. He forced himself to his feet, and the cold lashed at him. Trying to knock him down. Trying to make him bow. The world, and its men and gods, had always sought to make him bow.

Instead, Lukas laughed.

And when he could no longer laugh, he slumped. He was tired. He wanted this to be over. One way or another. He sat on his haunches, waiting. His least twitch was echoed and redoubled, swelling to fill the emptiness. He turned, studying the way he'd come. The path he'd taken was clear, his deep-set tracks marring the snow. Sweat steamed on his body, filling the air with his scent. His trail was obvious. Even a blind man could follow it.

'I know you're there,' he said, softly.

Know*know*there*there* came the echo. It mingled with the fading echoes of his laughter, to give the impression that something, somewhere, found this situation amusing.

'Push on, boy. Push on, before it catches up.'

He turned, listening. There were many voices on the wind. But this one was familiar. He shook his head. 'Kveldulf – go away, you're dead.'

'Do I look dead, boy? On your feet, we've leagues to go yet, and this meat won't carry itself. Up. Up!'

He scraped the ice from his eyes. Kveldulf was as he remembered, tall and iron-haired, with his plaited beard and hauberk of dragon-hide. Kveldulf, who bore the scars of a troll's claws on his face. Kveldulf, who'd been ripped open and strung like a red trail across the white by a trick of the light. The phantom crouched, blood from his wounds pooling beneath him. Kveldulf grinned. Bone shone through the ragged tatters of his cheek. 'There, boy. Pick it up.' A gore-stained finger pointed. The elk lay on the ice, steam rising from it still. 'Get that on your shoulders and let's go. The others are waiting.'

He remembered the elk. He remembered tracking it, with Kveldulf and the others, for three rises of the moon, into the north wind. Following spots and splashes of blood. 'It ran us a good race, boy, but nothing escapes us,' Kveldulf said. 'Up now. The tribe needs meat. Can't let them starve, boy, even if they do throw rocks at you on occasion.'

'You never threw rocks at me.'

'No. But I thought about it. Up.'

He pushed himself up. Kveldulf was right. The tribe needed meat. They had been counting on the hunters. The season had been bad for them. The sea ate their island home bite by bite as the weather turned and the waters rose. No man knew how much the landscape would change with the turning of the season, and solid ground was an illusion. The sea had its due eventually, and inexorably.

His childhood had been spent aboard ship, as the tribe navigated across the icy waters. It had been a savage, sea-borne existence – grinding, deadly tedium, broken by moments of sheer terror. When they'd finally found a scrap of rock to call their own, little had changed. They'd exchanged many-tentacled things with razor-beaks for ice trolls, and drowning for starvation. It was all faintly ridiculous. Lukas had learned to laugh early, and often. The others hadn't understood. They hadn't got the joke.

'We fought so hard, and for what?' Lukas said. 'A bit of rock that will sink into the sea sooner or later, and carry all of us with it, that's what.' He looked around. The elk was gone. So was Kveldulf. 'You weren't here,' he said. He wanted to howl. Kveldulf was dead. They were all dead. Killed by a trick of the light, with only him to tell the tale.

And that was the cruellest joke of all. Because no one would ever hear it, and even if they did, no one would believe him. He'd told too many stories, made too many boasts, to ever be believed in anything he said. Lukas Lie-Tongue. The son of a witch and a pickled corpse. Fit only for bedding women, avoiding work and being pelted with stones.

'Not a bad life,' he said, half-hoping Kveldulf would come back to tell him how wrong he was.

When no reply came, he shook his head and pushed on. The only sound was the crunch of snow. It echoed strangely, hesitantly. Crunch*crunch*. As if someone were stepping on his shadow. He wanted to turn, but he didn't want Kveldulf to yell at him again. The tribe was counting on them. They needed meat. It was soon to be the Time of Ice and Fire, and they would have to move, to flee the rising waters and seek higher ground.

Only the tribe had already moved. And Kveldulf was dead. It had been months since the others had died. Months into the season of upheaval, when the ice melted and the seas rose. He clutched at his head, trying to shake his thoughts into coherency. What was the past, and what was the present? The wolf in him growled. For beasts, all time was the present.

'But I'm not a beast, am I?' he said. 'Not yet.' His grip tightened, drawing blood. The pain was good. It brought clarity with it.

He knew who he was, where he was. And he knew why. This was a test of worth. The second test of Morkai, the great two-headed wolf who guarded the gates of the underworld. The Sky Warriors were testing him. To see if he deserved a place among them. And so they had forced a wolf into his belly, and cast him out into the wilds of Asaheim, to see if the beast chewed its way free of his flesh.

'Those the Canis Helix does not kill, it transforms forevermore.'

A rough voice, like the crash of waves against the hull of a ship. He looked up, into the wise, ancient eyes of the Rune Priest who had overseen his first test, when he'd first stepped through the Gates of Morkai. The Sky Warrior loomed over him, taller than even Kveldulf and thrice as broad in his frost grey war-plate and thick robes of wolf-fur. Bone fetishes and runestones were set into the crannies of his armour, and each one crackled with untold power. A face like carved wood, inset with gleaming yellow stones for eyes, glared down at him, in judgement.

'There is a shadow on your trail.'

Lukas looked down at his shadow. 'So I see.'

'No, you don't. Your mind is strong, though your body is frail. But what good is strength against the fire inside? For that is what we have awakened. Will you walk free, or be consumed?'

'And who asked you to stir it up?' Lukas spat. His jaw ached. He could feel the bones warping and thickening. His teeth split and flowered into fangs. He closed his eyes, trying to force down the rising heat. 'I was quite happy to die on the ice.'

The Rune Priest frowned and leaned on his staff. The runes etched into its length blazed like thousands of tiny stars. 'That is not your decision to make.'

Lukas stopped, swaying. 'That's where you are wrong. I can die here if I wish.'

The Rune Priest didn't answer. He wasn't there any longer, if he ever had been. Lukas pawed at his face, trying to resist the urge to simply... sit. Sit and wait. 'Death will be along, by and by,' he murmured. A saying of Kveldulf's. Very fatalistic, Kveldulf. Lukas could see the appeal, just now. He looked towards the horizon, and the distant stretch of rock that was the Fang. Were his tormentors watching him? He wanted nothing more than spite them, to show them the folly of forcing their demands upon him.

'I'll just sit here and freeze,' he said. 'If you want me, you'll have to come and get me.' An empty threat. They wouldn't come. They didn't care, not really. The old wolf had explained that much, at least.

Thought of the Wolf Priest made him snarl again. That grim ancient, with eyes like fire, made Lukas want to keep going, if only so he could spit in the old wolf's face. Memories burst across his mind, like barely healed scars tearing open. Of lying in the snow, his blood pumping from deep wounds, his mind slowing, drifting into the mists of death.

It had all gone wrong. From the moment that they had set out, their luck had been bad. The elk had proven stronger than their aim, and had led them a faltering chase across melting ice and up into the wild places. They'd followed, because what else could they do? They'd tracked it to its place of dying, only to discover that another hunter had beaten them to it. One who'd been in no mood to share.

Egyl had died first. Killed in the moment of discovery, his screams cut short as the snow swallowed him up. The others had followed, one at a time, until only Lukas remained, struggling on, fleeing south to the imagined safety of the tribe. Their killer had stalked him for days, following as close as his own shadow, until, at last, it had struck – and he had struck back. He'd sworn to whatever gods might be listening to take its pelt, if they would just give him the strength to do so. His blood and that of the beast had mingled on the snow as they fought, and it had fled, leaving him where he lay. He had been unable to move, for the pain. Things had been broken in him, or else torn loose from their moorings.

It had been a good death. Not the sort he would've preferred, but a fine death regardless. A worthy passing, if unseen. Only it hadn't been unseen. There had been an observer to the entire ordeal, from Egyl's passing to Lukas' last stand. As he'd lain there, leaking out his life, he'd felt a tremor pass through the ground. The crunch of ice and rock as something heavy strode towards him, out of the snow. Something black and massive, like a shard of night made flesh.

Red eyes had glowered down at him. Red eyes, set into a helm of bone and metal, a helm in the shape of a wolf's snarling muzzle. A gauntlet of black metal had reached down and caught up his broken body, despite his weak protests. A Chooser of the Valiant, claiming his soul. 'You could have chosen any of them,' Lukas said, to the snow. 'Instead, you chose me. You must be feeling very foolish, just about now.'

As if in answer, the wind rose, blistering his flesh. Shards of ice pricked his eyes and stung his breath from him. His shadow stretched back for leagues, drawn out by the sun. For the moment, he fancied he had two shadows. He listened to the wind and his breath, and the echoes of his movements. Crunch*crunch*.

'Why are you stopping, Lukas?' Gunnhild hissed, so close he almost jumped out of his skin. Her face was red, worn raw by the cold and wind. Her eyes were wide. Scared. They were all scared, though he was the only one to admit it. He laughed about it, but the others didn't. They couldn't see the humour.

'I heard it,' he said. 'It's behind us.'

'It's been behind us for days. We have to keep going.' Gunnhild spoke forcefully. She was forceful in everything she did. Older, sweeter memories slipped to the surface, and he brushed them aside. Now wasn't the time.

'If we could just *see* it…'

'Keep moving.' She grabbed one of his plaits and yanked on it. 'We have to keep moving or we'll wind up like Kveldulf and the others. The blink-devil will take us too.' Lukas looked at her, trying to focus. There was blood on her furs. There was blood everywhere. On her face. She was still talking, but he couldn't hear her over the wind. But he could hear the echoes of his footsteps, and he could hear his second shadow.

When Lukas looked back, Gunnhild was gone. He almost called out for her, as he had then. And like then, it would have been wasted breath. The blink-devil left no survivors. Those it hunted, vanished. All save him.

Why had he alone survived?

Unseen, something snarled. He turned. His heart – his hearts? – thumped and rattled against his ribs, like a wild beast in a cage. The sound might have come from beside him, or many miles away. Volcanic fury welled up in him, savage and insistent. He scanned the white, hunting his second shadow. Wanting to leap, to tear.

But there was nothing, save the wind and the light of the sun on the snow and the ice. He closed his eyes, trying to still the rage, to calm himself. He laughed. It was more like a growl. That only made him laugh harder. Lukas wondered what Gunnhild would make of him now, naked and laughing in the snow?

'She'd throw a rock at me,' he said, as he turned back.

It wasn't his fault that he had a sense of humour. If the

gods did not expect him to make use of it, why give it to him? Unless they too liked a good joke.

'No, that's not it,' he mumbled. He'd met the gods, and they were a humourless lot. He had seen the halls of Russ, and the high crags of Asaheim, though he'd never dreamed of, or wanted, such a thing. He was not the stuff of sagas. He was not a hero, not a Sky Warrior, no matter what the old wolf believed.

He was Lukas Lie-Tongue. He was boastful and foolish. He was a champion of japes and jests, not war. He had only been on the hunt because he'd infuriated one husband too many, and needed some time away. Kveldulf had dragged him by his ankle out of bed – not his own – and through the snow, lecturing him the entire way. The older warrior had taken Lukas in hand after his parents had died, reasoning that someone needed to. He hadn't done a very good job, but at least he'd tried. It was more than Lukas could say for some.

'You hear me, old wolf?' he growled. 'You made a mistake.' Lukas did not know the Wolf Priest's name, and he was certain that the old wolf didn't know his. Nor, he suspected, did the old wolf care. What did the gods care for the names of mortal men? 'You'll know my name before I'm done, though. Whatever comes.'

As if in reply to his boast, the white wavered. The ground was shaking. A tremor. Not unusual for this time of year. Lukas heard ice grinding and water sloshing. He leapt an instant before the ground split, and slammed into the fang of ice as it pierced the way ahead. Water spewed upwards with a crackling roar, and a blanket of cold enveloped him. He sprang for stable ground. He would have to run.

Despite his fatigue, he moved fast, springing from ice-chunk to ice-chunk until he was within sight of solid ground. The last spar of ice began to crack under him, and he prepared himself to make one final leap. His hearts were hammering. It wasn't fear. Not really. It was frustration – the thought of dying here, like this, drove him on. Maybe that was why the old wolf had left him out here – to die.

The ice exploded upwards, ejecting a profusion of slippery tentacles, encrusted with barnacle-like growths of bone. They snagged him as he leapt, tightening about his limbs. He was jerked down into the water with bone-rattling force. The cold water hit him like a fist, and then he was twisting down, caught in a deadly net of flesh.

Kraken mostly kept to the depths of the sea. But sometimes, when the waters rose, one swam inland, only to become caught in whatever shallow basin or lake it found itself in when the waters inevitably receded. These unlucky beasts often starved, unless they were fortunate enough to happen across prey. Like, say, a lone warrior stumbling across the ice, distracted by memories and ghosts.

Lukas cursed, filling the cold water with a flurry of bubbles. He tore an arm free of the thrashing coils and grabbed hold of a bone spur, holding it back from impaling him. His blood billowed, clouding the water. Through the veil of red, he saw a razored beak roughly the size of a man rising towards him. Eyes like torches flickered greedily in the depths. It was a small one, thank the Allfather. If it had been full sized he would have had no chance at all. A tentacle coiled about his throat, bone hooks digging painfully into his flesh. He lashed out with his feet, first jerking them free and then kicking away the slashing tentacles. A blow caught him on the back of the head and sent him spinning.

For a moment his mind turned to broken glass. Memories pricked at him, overwhelming him. Gunnhild laughing, screaming… dying. The feel of hard rocks against his back as the old wolf dragged his bloody carcass to the foot of the Fang and left him there for the thrall-servitors to collect. Even then, he'd been underestimated. They had expected him to expire before his training could begin. But he lived, if only to spite them. Lukas had never done as others expected, and he wasn't about to begin now.

A coil tightened convulsively about his other arm, and he felt his bones creak in protest. The pain startled him from his reverie. Snarling, he ducked his head and buried his fangs in the tentacle. Bilious ichors flooded his mouth and throat as he savaged the unnatural flesh. As he'd hoped, it released him. But not for long. Bone hooks slashed down, tearing at him. Kraken were relentless, once provoked. They would cheerfully fight larger monsters, just for a scrap of flesh.

Lukas kicked and flailed, trying to thrash a gap in the weaving thicket of tentacles that sought to bar his escape. His much-enlarged lungs strained as bludgeon-like blows struck him from all sides. He needed to get clear. He caught a blow on his forearm, letting the hooks dig into the meat and muscle, and sank the newly grown claws of his free hand into the tentacle. He braced his feet against the serpentine length and bit the kraken again. The wounded limb spasmed and swept out, carrying him with it.

Lukas snapped loose of the tentacle and tumbled slowly through the water. The kraken undulated after him. He began to swim for the dim light above, as quickly as his aching limbs could manage.

The kraken rose beneath him. The tips of its beak touched the soles of his feet, and he braced himself as its momentum carried them both out of the water. Lukas flipped through the air as the kraken twisted in its frenzy. Its beak snapped shut, just shy of his torso. He plummeted back down towards the ice. The kraken fell after him.

The ice nearly buckled beneath them. Lukas rolled aside as a tentacle slammed down over the spot where he'd landed. Out of the water, he could more easily discern the kraken's shape, and the squirming mass of its body. It was a yellowish colour, stripped with jagged markings of bluish green. Panting, he cast about for a weapon. He spotted a sliver of ice, as long and as thick as a spear, jutting up nearby. It would have to do. He sprang towards it, hoping to reach it before the kraken recovered.

The monster was wheezing like a bellows, its eyes rolling wildly in their filmy sockets. It heaved itself towards him, beak snapping. Bone-hooks thunked down, anchoring it as it hauled itself along. The ice was splintering beneath its weight. Lukas knew that if he didn't act soon, he'd be right back in the water, at the creature's mercy.

His hand closed around the splinter of ice and he wrenched it up, turning just as a trio of tentacles slapped down at him. He dodged one, rolling, and backpedalled away from the second, fighting to hold onto his makeshift spear. The third snared his ankle and jerked him into the air.

The kraken made a sound like the shriek of tearing metal and forced itself up, triangular head rising, beak wide open. It intended to swallow him before it slipped back into the water. He twisted in its grip, nearly popping his trapped leg from its socket. It released him, and he tumbled towards its open mouth. As he fell, he hurled the splinter of ice at one of the lamp-like eyes with all the force he could muster. Then the beak was closing about him, seeking to grind and pierce him. He caught the dorsal mandible on his palms and managed to brace his feet against the ventral, holding them open.

The saw-edged inner curve of the beak bit into his flesh, eliciting fresh agonies. The kraken was thrashing about, squealing in what he hoped was pain. Its muscles jerked and the pressure on his limbs increased.

Strong as he was, he wasn't capable of holding the monster's mouth open forever. Already, the beating he'd taken was wearing him down. Sweat stung his eyes. Lukas swung his head, looking for an escape route. Only one presented itself. With a curse that was almost a howl, Lukas thrust his arms and legs out to their fullest extension, momentarily dislocating the kraken's jaws. He seized the opportunity to throw himself down its gullet. He could've risked heading for open air, but the chance of the beak snapping shut on him was too great to ignore. This way, he at least had a hope of staying in one piece.

The kraken's throat was a narrow tube of rigid cartilage, lined with curved blades of bone. Lukas snapped several of these off as he slid down, inflicting more damage on himself as he did so. He wrenched one free of its mooring and began to hack at the cartilage with increasing desperation. The kraken was writhing in agony, and gusts of hot air rose up from beneath him, bathing him in an oily stench. He knew that he had to tear himself a hole before the monster managed to heave itself back into the water. When he'd succeeded in creating a crack, he forced the spine of bone into it and levered it into widening further.

He sank his fingers into the wound and began to pull. A low, throbbing sound pulsed upwards, like the reverberations of some unseen bell, and he began to wrench and jerk at the cartilage, until the gap was at last wide enough to accommodate his shoulders. Burning torrents of ichor poured over him as he forced himself into the gap. Rubbery purple flesh lay beyond and he tore at it with his teeth and fingers. There was a sound like sailcloth tearing, and then a blast of arctic cold washed over him.

Lukas, accompanied by a gout of ichor, sprawled on the ice, gasping. Behind him, the kraken made a choked, gurgling sound that resonated through his bones, and then collapsed. It tentacles squirmed, striking at everything in its death throes. Lukas scrambled out of the way, lungs heaving.

'Bit off more than you could chew, eh?' he said, falling onto his back. He watched the kraken's final moments with dull interest. When it at last grew still, he realised that his stomach was rumbling.

It wasn't an elk, but it would do.

The change his body was undergoing was akin to a fire that needed constant fuel. He tore a tentacle free of the carcass and began to gorge on the rubbery, possibly toxic, flesh. As he assuaged his hunger, he noted that his spear of ice had struck its target – one of the creature's eyes was gone, burst in a welter of gelid muck. But so too was the other eye. Something had torn the semi-luminescent orb from its socket and left it squashed on the ice. There were gouges on the kraken's skull and what looked to be bite-marks on its tentacles.

Something had attacked the monster, even as it tried to devour him. The marks were familiar – indeed, he had similar scars on his own hide. Lukas grinned around a mouthful of kraken. 'So that's the way it is,' he mumbled. He snatched a handful of snow from the ground and thrust it into his mouth. As it melted, he swallowed it, enjoying the soothing coolness. He'd screamed himself raw, fighting the beast. He sniffed the air, scenting nothing but the ichors of the kraken.

But the creature was nearby. It had been on his trail all along, following him at a careful distance. He wondered if it had been surprised, when it had caught his scent. Probably. He chuckled.

'A good joke,' he said. 'Dropping me there. A good joke, old wolf.' The old wolf had left Lukas where he'd first found him. Where the blink-devil had almost claimed him. He looked around, but saw nothing save falling snow and water vapour. 'A very good joke,' he said again, more quietly this time.

'You and your damn jokes.'

'It's not my fault you have no sense of humour, Thord,' Lukas said. Thord crouched in the snow, his intestines pooling around his ankles. Like Kveldulf and Gunnhild, Thord was dead. Meat for the beast, his complaints stifled by crushing jaws.

'Quiet, Smiler. It's out there… watching us.' Thord didn't look at him. Lukas was thankful. No one should have to see his cousin's face stripped to bloody bone. Thord's wounds were dripping, turning the white snow pink.

'Let it,' Lukas said, still chewing on a mouthful of kraken. 'Let it watch, let it follow.'

'If not for your jokes, we would not be here, Smiler,' Thord said, accusingly. Smiler. The name some of Lukas' kin had given him. They spat it like a curse. As if a smile were a weakness. As if good humour were the flaw in otherwise strong iron. Don't joke, Smiler. Don't laugh, Smiler. Don't, don't, don't.

His kin had always tried to impose their will on him, to force him into the shape they dictated. And he had ever escaped that fate, if only by the skin of his teeth. They wanted a warrior, he became a lover. They wanted stern, and he laughed at every opportunity. They thought him a coward, and he fought with animal fury, when pressed. He was not snow, to be packed and shaped. He was fire, rising and falling as it willed. He met Thord's cloudy gaze.

'If not for my jokes, Thord, we would be somewhere worse,' he said.

'We would be home.'

'As I said.' Lukas dipped his head to take a bite.

When he looked up, Thord was gone. Like Gunnhild. Like Kveldulf. Gone. He closed his eyes, remembering. Kveldulf had died third, after Egyl and Harada. They had become lost after that. And one by one, they'd all gone, save him. Vanishing into the white, lost to snow and ice. Lost to the blink-devil.

That was what his people called it. Other tribes had other names for the beasts, but blink-devil described it well enough. The beasts were shapeshifters and lightbenders. They were never where you thought, and never looked the same way twice. According to the stories he'd heard as a boy, they were always behind you, no matter which way you turned. They moved in the blink of an eye, and between breaths. They hid in men's shadows, and lurked just out of sight.

Worst of all, they had a sense of humour. They would trail their prey for days, weeks, even months, harrying it to the point of exhaustion and madness before they struck for the final time. The common wisdom was that when one caught your scent, it was best to just cut to the chase and gut yourself.

Lukas had considered that, after it had taken Gunnhild, if only to spite the beast. He'd been alone then. But he'd always been alone, after a fashion. Part of the tribe, but separate. But the blink-devil had taken even that from him. And he'd resolved to take its life, in recompense. A bitter smile crept across his face.

'Only that didn't work out, did it?' he said. His words echoed back at him, and the kraken meat in his belly turned sour.

The ice suddenly dipped, as the weight of the kraken's corpse finally caused it to shatter. The mass slid into the water, nearly dragging Lukas with it. He leapt back, scrabbling for the rising edge of the ice. His fingers and toes found cracks and he pulled himself up, hand over hand, until he was balanced on the edge.

He took a steadying breath, and leapt. The reverberations of the kraken's sinking stretched outwards, pursuing him as he dropped to the next floe of ice and began to run.

Head down, Lukas pelted for solid ground. His limbs pumped, carrying him to safety. The cracks pursued him for longer than he liked to think about, zigzagging in his wake. He leapt over them when they crossed his path, and tried to outpace them.

When the ground at last stopped trembling and the ice subsided, he allowed himself to sink down, panting. He could barely hear the wind over the rushing of his blood. He looked up, trying to spy the way ahead. The snow was falling more thickly now. A black shape watched him from a ridge of ice and stone many leagues away. He blinked. He could see further now, but even so, he could just barely make out the hulking shape, clad in thick furs, standing amongst the scrub trees. He recognized it regardless. The old wolf was watching him. He forced himself to his feet, chest heaving.

'Feel free to applaud,' Lukas shouted, casting his voice into the teeth of the wind.

Snow swirled, obscuring his vision. When it cleared, the shape was gone. He threw back his head and laughed. 'You'll miss the best part.' His words did not echo. The snow swallowed them up. He took a step.

Crunch*crunch*.

Lukas shifted, tensing. 'Is this it, then?' he said. 'Kraken not to your taste, perhaps?'

Crunch*crunch*.

He whipped around, bare fist hissing through snow. He thought – just for a moment – that he'd touched something. Then it was gone. He could hear the sound of ice cracking. And voices on the wind. He clutched himself, as the thing inside him surged up, rocking his frame with its exertions. It wanted to be free, to hunt.

'Can't hunt what you can't see, fool,' he hissed, through clenched teeth. He'd learned that the hard way. They all had. One by one, the blink-devil had taught them to fear the unseen. All except him. He'd taught it to fear *him*.

It came back in a rush. The stink of blood, the too-sweet odour of its oily hide. A glint of fang. The sound of claws sinking into flesh, tearing. And the weight of his knife. He'd let it get close, let it show itself, thinking him worn down. And then he'd seen the colour of its blood, spattering the snow. How it had shrieked!

It had underestimated him. It wasn't alone in that. Everyone underestimated him, even the gods. They'd left him out here, naked and alone. His hands flexed. He wished he had his knife, something, anything to cut with. Claws were fine, but he wasn't yet a beast...

Out in the white, wolves howled. Or maybe not wolves. He wasn't alone out here. He wasn't the only one being tested by the Allfather. Part of him wanted to join them, to throw back his head and howl. Howl until the ghosts left him alone. Howl until there was nothing left of him but the red wolf nestled in his gut. But he still had a hunt to finish. He set his feet back on the path to the Fang and began to walk.

'That's what this is all about, isn't it?' he muttered, talking both to himself as well as the creature lurking just out of sight. He remembered the heat of the great fiery rivers which ran to either side of the Gate of Morkai, down in the roots of the Fang. He remembered the apprehension which had gripped him, as he looked up into the dual muzzles of the wolf-god carved there over the portal; the worry that he was truly as unfit as he believed, and that all his days were done. That he'd been saved from certain, if honourable, doom only to meet an ignoble end in the kingdom of the gods.

He laughed. 'And wouldn't that have been the perfect end to a perfect life?' But it hadn't ended there. Determined to be done with it all, for good or ill, he had braved the gate, and found the Rune Priest waiting for him there. They had spoken at length, in the dark and quiet. About what, Lukas could not fully recall. And then had come the final test. The old wolf had come for him, and dragged him away. Had taken him out of the Fang and into the wilds and thrown him down onto the ice without a word.

'Right back where we started. And what's the point of that?' Lukas continued on, cursing the old wolf the entire time. He owed the old wolf, for taking him into the blizzard, to Asaheim. Owed him and hated him in equal measure. If he hadn't been watching...

'You would have died,' Kveldulf said, striding along to the right of him, one arm holding in his torn guts. 'Just like us, boy.' He gestured, blood dripping from his fingers. Lukas didn't have to look around to know Kveldulf hadn't come alone, this time. 'And wouldn't that have been the joke of a lifetime?'

Lukas stopped. 'You never really understood what a joke was, did you?'

'Too late to learn now, I suppose,' Kveldulf said.

Lukas looked away. 'He should have saved you.'

'Too old,' Kveldulf said. He looked down at his stomach. 'Who knew a body had so many guts in it? Like a coil of rope, unspooling across the snow.'

Lukas grimaced. 'Then he should have taken Thord, or Egyl, or Gunnhild...' He glared at the snow. 'One of the others.'

'And when have the gods ever chosen a woman to journey to Asaheim, you great dunce?' Gunnhild said, appearing to his left. She didn't sound bitter, merely amused. 'Outside of those vulgar stories of yours, I mean.'

'I'd have gone, but you got me killed,' Thord said. He stood in Lukas' path, flanked by the others; indistinct faces blotted out by the snow and his own failing memories. The tribulations he had undergone had weakened his recall, layering new lessons over the old. Lukas glared at his cousin.

'Go to Hel, Thord.'

'Already there, Smiler.' Thord held his hands out, letting his wounds gape open and his insides bulge out like startled serpents. Lukas laughed.

'You dropped something.'

Thord grimaced. Then he was gone. Lukas wondered if ghosts sulked.

Behind him, something growled. Softly, softly. A susurrus of intent. Lukas crouched, muscles tensing, teeth bared. No wonder Thord had left. Something slunk through the snow, circling him. Keeping its distance. How long had it been following him? Hours? Days? He shook his head. How long had he been out here?

'Not long enough.'

The voice was guttural, like ice floes colliding in a storm-tossed sea. The old wolf stalked beside him, war-plate creaking. He left no prints in his wake, despite his weight. 'Not long enough to learn respect. To learn that you are nothing but what the Allfather chooses to make of you, pup.'

The Wolf Priest had refused to call him by name, as if Lukas were not worthy of such familiarity. 'You're not worth anything,' the old wolf said, reading the look on his face. 'Not yet. Not until you join the pack.'

'Who says I want to join?'

The old wolf grunted. 'The Allfather.'

'Your Allfather watched them die,' Lukas said, his fingers curling into fists. His new claws gouged wounds in his palms. He knew the old wolf wasn't here. He was just another trick of the light, like Kveldulf and Gunnhild. A phantom sent to torment him. To test him. Regardless, he would say his piece. 'You watched, and they died. You could have done something.'

'I did.'

'Besides that,' Lukas growled.

'I am not your nursemaid, pup. I did my duty. I am a Chooser of the Valiant.'

'Then you chose poorly.'

The old wolf was silent. Then, 'Maybe so. But we will not know until you fail.'

Lukas smiled. 'I'm tempted to let it kill me, just so I can see the look on your face.'

'If you are dead you will see nothing at all, save the jaws of Morkai as he feasts on your soul,' the old wolf said, his voice as deep as the sea, from shore to shore.

Lukas stepped back, unnerved despite himself. 'I don't understand this.'

'You do not have to understand.'

Lukas felt he'd had this conversation before. He shook his head. 'Shut up. You're not here. Just a trick of the light. A trick of my weakness.' He laughed and closed his eyes. 'For that matter, am I even here? Perhaps I still stand in the Gate of Morkai, dreaming, as the Rune Priest digs through my mind.'

When he opened his eyes, the old wolf was gone. Lukas snorted. That was gods for you… never around when you needed them. But now that he'd made his appearance, perhaps this saga was coming to its close. Behind him, something growled softly. He heard the whisper of heavy paws, treading on his tracks. He was hurt. Bleeding. Weak. Lukas smiled thinly. The blink-devil was clever. It had been waiting for him to tire, to grow weary. The kraken must've surprised it. It had thought the creature was stealing its prey, and had attacked like any enraged predator. The way it had attacked Egyl, at the beginning of all of this.

'And here is the lesson,' Lukas said. 'All of it – an accident. A mistake from beginning to end.'

'And thus you betray your foolishness.'

Lukas turned. A different Sky Warrior now. Not the old wolf, but the Rune Priest again in his bone charms and rune-etched war-plate, a stern look on his ancient face. Lukas grinned.

'Come back for another chat?'

'There is a spark in you, pup. A spark which may yet be fanned into a flame of greatness.'

Lukas laughed. 'No one has ever accused me of being great.' This was the same conversation they'd had beneath the Gate of Morkai, he thought, though he couldn't be sure. Were these hallucinations, or memories? Or maybe both. Maybe this moment and that were all one. Wolves experienced only the present. For them, past and future blended into an eternal now. Why should it be any different for these wolves, though they walked on two legs rather than four? What did time mean to an immortal, after all?

'No, I expect not.' Thin lips twisted in a mirthless smile. The Rune Priest shook his head. 'Then, in the eyes of the All-father, even the least of us might yet prove our worth before the Wolf Time.'

Lukas stopped. He could feel the sea surging deep beneath the ice. 'And is that what this is all about, then? Me proving my worth?'

'It is a test. All of it. From the moment of your birth, to the

method of your dying.' The Sky Warrior stared down at him.
'That is what you do not understand, pup.'

'I understand,' Lukas said, resisting the urge to snarl. 'But I
don't like it.'

'It is not up to you to like it. Merely to accept it, and perse-
vere. Such is the will of the Allfather.'

'How do you know?'

'He speaks to us.'

'He must do so very quietly, because I've never heard him.'

The blow came so suddenly, that Lukas was on his hands and
knees before he registered it. He wheezed and clutched at his
chest. His palm came away bloody. The skin of his torso was
marred by claw marks. The Sky Warrior was gone. Something
else, infinitely preferable for all its hostility, was in his place.

'Well then,' Lukas growled, thrusting himself to his feet.
'Finally.' He lunged. He was off-balance, and the movement
was awkward.

Even so, he got a handful of greasy fur. Claws tore along his
ribs and back as the blink-devil leapt on him, biting and tearing. He couldn't see it properly. It vanished, spilling his blood
and dancing away with an eager whine. His nerves caught
up with the damage and he staggered. Vibrant streaks of red
sluiced down his shoulders and flanks, staining the snow.

'You remember me, don't you?' he gasped. 'I've only ever
been hit like that by people I've personally offended. You must
have taken that stabbing personally.'

All was silent, save for the susurrus of the snow. But it was
still there, still circling him, watching him, jaws sagging. It had
a taste of him now and wouldn't flee again. He was grateful
for that – for a chance at a proper ending to things. 'Yes, you
took it personally, didn't you? They always take it personally.'

Suddenly dizzy, he sank to one knee. The ice spun about

him. His limbs felt like leaden weights and his blood made rosettes on the snow. 'Just like before,' he said, chuckling harshly. 'Only no knife, now. And I've been chewed up and spat out by a kraken.' He ducked his head, and peered surreptitiously at his shadow. Just the one, for the moment. That would change. 'But you're still afraid, aren't you? That's why I'll have the last laugh – that's why I survived, when the others died. Someone has to laugh over your lonely grave, beast, and who better than me?' He turned in place, arms spread, inviting attack. Hoping for it. 'The gods interrupted us last time. They bought us both a little time to prepare for this moment, but that's done now. So let's get to it.'

Out in the snow, something snarled. He fancied he heard an element of frustration in that sound. Of gratification long-delayed. How long had it hunted him? How long had it lingered here, with the taste of his blood in its mouth and the ache of his blade in its flesh? It had followed him across cracking ice and through frost-shrouded forests, down valleys and up mountains. And for what? Had the gods truly known, or was this simply fate? Was it truly the same creature, or was he simply deluding himself into seeing an end to his story where there was none?

'No,' he said, smiling. 'Not even the gods are that cruel. To deny one of us, certainly. But both – never.' His smile vanished as the blink-devil lunged at him again, vaulting out of the snow onto his back. He was knocked flat by its weight. Teeth dug into the back of his neck, but only for an instant. He threw his head back, and felt bone crunch. His attacker yelped and retreated, too swiftly for him to follow.

Lukas rolled to his feet. He touched his neck, and felt wetness. He was a mass of wounds, none of them debilitating as yet. But each one slowed him down just a bit more. And the creature was fast. Faster than him, even if he hadn't been injured, and maybe stronger. It was hungry, and hunger lent it ferocity. He knew the feeling. Whatever strength he'd drawn from the kraken was almost used up.

He tried to spot the blink-devil in the snowfall, but it was impossible to focus on for any length of time. He couldn't see it clearly, no matter how much he squinted. There were three of it, and then five and then none. It flickered in and out of sight, becoming snow, rock and other things. It was disorientating, like trying to fight a nightmare. Every blow he launched passed through where it had been. It wasn't changing shape – not really. It merely reflected your perceptions back at you. It showed you what you expected to see.

Claws tore furrows in his back, and he stumbled forward, cursing. It had got behind him, somehow. He was stronger than he had been, and tougher. But the creature was stronger still. Jaws fastened in the meat of his calf, and he was yanked off balance. He fell face down, busting his nose. He kicked out with his free foot, and felt something give beneath the wild blow. The blink-devil rolled away, yelping.

Lukas dragged himself to his feet, limping now.

'Come on,' he growled. 'Is that it? You got a taste before. Come have the full meal.' He could smell its stink on the air, growing stronger and fading away again, as if it were drawing close and then retreating. It was a wary beast. Even now, drawn by the scent of his familiar blood. He wondered if his blows had hurt it – or maybe it had been injured by the kraken, earlier. 'Here I stand, beast... alone, bleeding, freezing. I'm here. Come and get me.'

Out of the corner of his eye, he glimpsed familiar faces. The dead were watching him. Kveldulf, Gunnhild... even Thord. They had all gathered to watch this moment, their faces set, grim. Even now, they refused to laugh. Lukas shook his head, trying to clear it. 'Let's give them a show, shall we?'

'This is not a joke,' the Rune Priest said. Lukas couldn't see him, but heard his voice as if the Sky Warrior were looming just behind him. Lukas licked his teeth, tasting his own blood.

'I disagree,' he said, simply. Another test. It was all a test, of him, of his worth. Perhaps, as he'd joked, he was not on the ice, was not truly facing the creature that had killed his friends and kin. Perhaps it was all in his head. He laughed. 'No. If this were in my head, you'd be a woman, old devil. Or a table, groaning with food and drink. And I'd have trousers on, at least. But it's the same test, isn't it?'

The Test of Morkai. Two tests in one. 'Two heads, same wolf,' Lukas said. He laughed again, relishing in the sound. 'That's a good joke, isn't it?' He tapped the side of his head as he turned, trying to follow the blink-devil's movements. 'They make you think it's two, but it's all the same test, to see if you're worthy. And it never ends, does it? They keep testing you, keep trying to make you fit, to force you into the grave they dug for you before you were even born. But I refuse to lay down for anyone but myself…'

The blink-devil came at him in a rush. Crunch*crunch*. The sound of its footsteps, in the echo of his own. It moved with him, breathed with him, growled with him. It was his shadow. Lukas blinked. He glanced down. He had two shadows now. He smiled. Crunch*crunchcrunch*. He spun, hands extending to catch hold of a hairy throat as something launched itself at him, out of a snow flurry.

'There you are,' he spat, as its momentum carried them both backwards. The ice cracked beneath them, and he rolled over, dragging the beast with him. Its fangs pierced the flesh of his forearm, and he tightened his grip on its throat, trying to throttle it. It had him pinned, its weight almost equal to his own. Even now, it could kill him, if he didn't kill it first. And even now, part of him hesitated. To kill it was to do as the gods wished, and he desperately wished to spite them, to show them that he was not their puppet.

The blink-devil snarled and the bones in his forearm cracked as its jaws tightened. Up close, he could see that it resembled a wolf, but only in the sense that it had four legs and a tail. It was as much a kraken, or an elk, as a wolf, as if some mad god had taken the most unpleasant bits from all of the other animals and tied them together with strings of malice. It was a shadow on clear ice, a shape seen out of the corner of the eye, a nightmare of fangs and claws and shimmering fur.

He felt no fear, staring into its mad, yellow eyes. Only a sense of purpose, of satisfaction long delayed. Here was the last, best moment of an ill-starred life. The gods thought this moment theirs, but it was his. They had given him the tools for victory, but it was still his hand which wielded them. He would kill the beast, but not for the Sky Warriors in their icy fastness. He would do it for Kveldulf, and Gunnhild and even Thord. He owed them that much. But mostly, he would do it for himself.

'You can't kill me, old devil… I was born dead,' he snarled. He jerked his bitten arm aside, yanking it off balance, exposing its neck. He buried his new-sprouted fangs in its hairy throat. It struggled, whining, and he wrapped his legs around its middle, trapping it. No more running. Its blood tasted bitter, and he drank deeply of it. Claws dug canyons into his chest and sides. It kicked at him, trying to disembowel him. He took the pain as he continued to savage its throat, tearing flesh and muscle, cracking bone. Laughing as he did so.

With a final kick, the blink-devil died. A shudder ran through its frame and it became a dead weight, pressing him against the ice. Lukas shoved the limp carcass aside and spat out a lump of gristle and sinew. Panting, he stared up at the sky.

'Did I win?' he said. 'I hope so, otherwise I'll never get to see the old wolf's disappointment.' He looked over at the blink-devil. It lay still and stiff, frost already collecting on its matted fur. Even dead, it was hard to perceive. Soon, it would vanish forever, and take his triumph with it.

He was tired. And cold.

Lukas rolled over, and crawled towards the creature. The wolf in him wanted to feed, to gorge on the cooling meat of his kill. But he had other priorities. 'I swore to the Allfather that I'd take your pelt, beast. Even I wouldn't go back on such an oath. So, off it comes. Now, hold still, eh?' Lukas caught a handful of the beast's pelt and began to slice it free from the body with his claws. It was rough going, but he managed.

'I feel as if there were easier ways of doing this,' he said, as he worked. 'A drinking contest, perhaps? Last man to the bottom of a cask loses. Or an eating contest. We always said that a man who could stomach Gunnhild's cooking was worthy of joining the gods.' He ignored the flash of pain her name caused. Gunnhild was dead.

'And you are not.'

Lukas looked up. The voice echoed in his head like distant thunder, and drove out the cold that clung to his bones. A golden figure, shining like the sun at the height of summer, was watching him. He could not make out its features, such was its radiance, but he recognized the being regardless.

'No, I'm not,' he said, his voice hoarse with fear, or perhaps hope. 'Why? Why choose me?'

The Allfather said nothing. Lukas peered up at him, waiting for him to do something. Anything. Then, softly, slowly, like the rumble of a distant avalanche, the Allfather chuckled.

Turned away. Vanished. As if he had never been. And maybe he hadn't. With such a being, it was impossible to say. Either way, Lukas had his answer.

His gods might not laugh. But their god certainly did.

Lukas' grin almost split his face. He bent to his task, and finished stripping the blink-devil of its fur. He stood and swung the dripping pelt over his shoulders. He looked down at the carcass. It was shrunken, somehow, in death. A thing broken by its own hubris. It had assumed itself the stronger, and seen him as prey. As the kraken had. But he had proven it wrong, even as he had proven his people wrong.

As he had proven the old wolf wrong.

Lukas looked around. The dead surrounded him, watching as the Allfather had. Then they too faded, one by one, until he stood alone on the ice. He missed them, but he was alive and they had gone somewhere he had no intention of going until the time of his choosing. He still had so much to do.

Wrapped in the skin of his shadow, Lukas continued his journey. And when he at last reached the base of the Fang, the old wolf was waiting for him, skull-helmet tucked beneath one arm.

'You still live,' the old wolf said, looking down at him.

'I do.'

'Mayhap your survival is a credit to me then, as well as yourself.' The old wolf grimaced as he examined the pelt Lukas wore. 'You slew the doppelgangrel, then.'

Lukas didn't have to ask what the Wolf Priest was referring to. 'You knew it was out there,' he said, without rancour.

'It was–'

'A test, yes,' Lukas said, his grin tight. The wolf in him snarled with fury, but he forced it back into its cage. 'To see if I was worthy.'

'Even so.'

'And I passed. The question I have now is… are you worthy of me?' Lukas was gratified to see a look of incomprehension pass over the old wolf's face. He pulled the blink-devil – no, the doppelgangrel – pelt tighter about himself, and he realised that it still held its glamour. The old wolf squinted at him, trying to focus.

'I saw in you the spirit of the wolf, and you have not proven me wrong.' One black gauntlet gestured to his trophy. 'Toss that filthy pelt aside. You no longer require it.'

'I think it suits me,' Lukas said. The gods saw the world in grey absolutes, but the world was more like the stinking fur he wore – ever changing. He wondered if perhaps that was why he had survived – not for vengeance, or to prove his own worth, but to test theirs. Perhaps that too was the Allfather's will.

Or maybe, he simply had a sense of humour.

The old wolf's grimace slid into an uncertain frown. 'Then keep it. And keep your scars as well. You've earned them. The Allfather welcomes you, pup.'

Lukas met the Wolf Priest's gaze unflinchingly.

'My name is Lukas,' he said.

And he laughed.

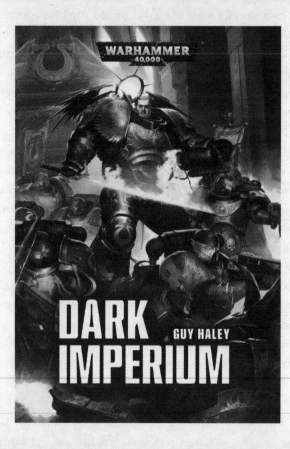

DARK IMPERIUM
by Guy Haley

The galaxy has changed. Darkness spreads, warp storms split reality and Chaos is everywhere – even Ultramar. As Roboute Guilliman's Indomitus Crusade draws to a close, he must brave the perils of the warp to reach his home and save it from the depredations of the Plague God.

Find this title, and many others, on blacklibrary.com

WARHAMMER
AGE OF SIGMAR

Bear Eater

David Guymer

The sun was searing bright, the sky a lens of crystal blue, shaped by gods for the glorification of their oasis of light. Towers of white stone with domed roofs of mosaic gold shone with a splendour that stole a man's breath, and drew sweat even from an immortal's brow. The trek across the Sea of Bones had been arduous, but dust and battle damage aside, the dozen Astral Templars still standing could outshine any Mortal Realm for glory.

Liberators in heavy armour of deep amethyst and gold marched in silent ranks; their shields were up in defiance of the sun, hammers strapped across their backs, heads high. The Prosecutors flanked them, walking in lockstep, but with the mechanisms of their wings unfurled, enhancing their size threefold. Their pinions sizzled with god-wrought might. To the rear came a pair of Judicators, the stocks of their crossbows each held in one heavy gauntlet, the stirrups to their shoulders. In the absence of the wrath of Azyr, the weapons were bright but otherwise inert arcs of blessed sigmarite. Impressive regard-less, their function plain enough to anyone who knew war.

Even they were but a foretaste.

Hamilcar Bear-Eater marched a stride ahead, his helmet carried under the crook of his arm. His face was tattooed and bearded, his thick pile of red hair sweaty under the desert sun. His teeth were painted black, and he grinned for the awed men and terrified children that lined the Sacred Mile of Jercho to witness the return of Sigmar. Stick-figure representations of sacred beasts marked the rugged sigmarite of his armour, sand-blasted, sun-faded, dim now as his own memory of the land and people that had spawned them. It clanked as he walked, the strapping loosened against the heat, his warding lantern banging on the opposite hip. A cloak of tattered Carthic bear-skin trailed limply over one shoulder.

Larger than life, men had once called him, when he too had still been a man.

What then, he wondered, could they call him now?

The soldiery of Jercho lined the approach in their finest war gear. They were armoured in short-sleeved leather lorica and skirts sewn with bronze plates. Masks of the same metal, cast in the likeness of a rising sun, covered the upper halves of their faces, eyes peering through slit holes, only their frowns visible. The exposed skin of their arms, legs and chins was the brown of baked bread. Several ranks stood flawlessly to attention under the punishing midday heat – the sun was always high over Jercho – a line of spearmen that ran the Sacred Mile all the way from the Gates of Noon and the citadel of Jercho itself. Archers with long composite bowstaves made of hewn-beam and grindworm tooth tracked the procession from the rooftops.

The Astral Templars were not the only ones intent on making an impression.

'There certainly are a lot of them,' muttered Broudiccan.

The Decimator-Prime was a man of heroic stature and few words, which was what Hamilcar, a man of many words of tremendous import, appreciated about him most. His helmet bore a dent from a battle with the sankrit, a reptilian people whose small empire straddled the northernmost reaches of the Sea of Bones. The sankrit had clawed knuckles, and the blow to Broudiccan's faceplate had left a deep gouge across the mask's impassive mouth that only deepened the warrior's gloomy aspect.

'There always are.' Hamilcar thumped his breastplate with a clenched fist, making one of the nearby spearmen start. 'There is only ever one of Hamilcar.' The granite-white gryph-hound, Crow, that padded alongside him growled in apparent assent, or perhaps in hunger as it considered the soldiers of Jercho.

'Think of what might be achieved if these people can be returned to Sigmar's fold,' said Thracius, last surviving Prime of his Liberators, his armour sand-polished and aglow with Sigmar's energy, his manner characteristically ebullient. 'Look upon Jercho's wealth. And these towers, so grand, earthly twins to those of Sigmaron herself! Two Mortal Realms have I waged holy war upon, Hamilcar, and never seen the like of Jercho – a nation of city-states, as yet unmarred by the Age of Chaos. Their confidence and power would be a boon to Sigmar's, equal to anything we have achieved in Ghur thus far.'

Ever restless, Hamilcar's mind turned back.

He had been dispatched to the Realm of Beasts to reconquer the cities of the Carthic Oldwoods and oversee their resettlement in Sigmar's name. He had succeeded, for Hamilcar always succeeded, only to see that great work undone as one by one those cities fell to marauding bands of ogors, the orruk hordes of the Great Red, and then, the deathblow, to the undying legions of Mannfred von Carstein.

It had been Mannfred that had slain him, in the final battle for once-mighty Cartha, and the ignominy of his defeat lingered more than the appalling injuries required to slay one as mighty as he. He was troubled, more often than he would admit, by dreams of that day. He would awake, clad in sweat, his halberd gripped so fiercely that if the dreams did not cease then one day even blessed sigmarite would snap. A lesser immortal would have broken, but it was not often that the gods forged men of Hamilcar's mettle. Aware, as a god must be, of the evil that plagued his greatest champion, Sigmar had granted him swift catharsis, giving him the vanguard of the bladestorm that had driven Mannfred from the Sea of Bones and, in alliance with the hosts of Arkhan the Black, broken the back of the Great Red. The quest to bring the vampire to heel went on, and, though it had aggrieved Lord-Relictor Ramus of the Hallowed Knights, there was none better than Hamilcar to pursue it.

It was not about vengeance. Nor was it even about restitution; in his heart he knew that the memory of his death would be with him to the end of days.

He was a hunter, and the vampire was his prey.

'The Hammers of Sigmar and the Celestial Vindicators claim the realms for Sigmar,' Broudiccan grumbled, 'while we battle half-sentient lizard people for an arid waste that no one desires and one worthless night-walker that time forgot to slay.'

'This is where the glory will be, brothers,' Hamilcar declared.

'What makes you so sure?'

Hamilcar spread his arms, his armour shining under the bright sun. The answer was so blindingly apparent that he did not need to speak it. He laughed instead, clapping Broudiccan on the pauldron so sparks of lightning played through the fingers of his gauntlet as he pushed his brother on.

Say one thing for Hamilcar Bear-Eater: he is not greedy with his glory.

The Knight-Heraldor, Frankos, sounded a note on his long, curved horn, the standard of the Knight-Vexillor held proudly aloft as Hamilcar and his best marched into the Plaza Solar.

The great plaza of marble and tinkling fountains was set in the sultry wind-shade of the citadel's ramparts. They were immense. The white stone of the walls was dazzling. The arrowslits were framed with gold. Fantastical banners of bright and daring colours fluttered against the bright blue sky, but the Solar itself felt no wind. The ornamental fountains sounded a note of coolness, but heat pressed down like a mailed fist.

Frankos' herald faded into the still air. Silence fell, breathless, with a clatter of sigmarite as Stormcasts shifted in their armour for relief from the heat.

Shielding his eyes, Hamilcar looked up the huge curtain walls to where a robed man with a bald head stood with his lips to a trumpet of gold-plated ivory. And there, on the highest rampart, surrounded by his banners and servants and beneath a shaded canopy, was the throne of Joraad el Ranoon.

The sun-king.

The king of Jercho was clad in a loose banyan of green silk, the hem and sleeve decorated with a chequer pattern of white and green. His arms were heavy with jewelled torques, his neck wound with heavy necklaces of gold. A golden mask that emitted rays like those of the sun covered his face in full, and a crown sat upon his head.

Joraad leaned forward and his voice, when he spoke, boomed from all around, hundreds of voices, echoing from the fine statuary and feminine caryatids of the Solar.

Hamilcar turned his gaze to see the men and women arrayed in royal livery above the square. He had been told of this.

The Rays of the sun-king: bonded by ritual magic to the will of their lord.

'I, Joraad, heir to the reign of Ranoon, regent of Jercho and king of earth and sky, welcome the embassy of Sigmar to my throne. Come in peace, brothers long lost, returned to us now by the blessings of the gods.'

A stilted breeze stirred the high banners. Hamilcar licked the salty dryness from his lips and squinted over the silent crowds. He had been expecting a cheer, a dutiful applause. Something.

'Why does he sit in shade while we bake?' Broudiccan murmured. 'Is he the sun-king or is he not?'

Chuckling at his brother's bleak humour, Hamilcar stepped forward. He let the quiet linger a moment longer. Then he took a deep breath; his lungs swelled, his diaphragm dropped.

Broudiccan and Thracius took a step back.

'And Sigmar's greeting to you!' His voice was a hammer beaten against the shieldwall of the sky. The pennants above the castle gatehouse fluttered. He looked up to the sun-king, eyes narrowed and shot through with red by the noon glare. 'We are the eternals of Azyr, and by the might of Sigmar we have returned!'

The sun-king peered down, nonplussed, appearing to remonstrate with one of his many fan-waving attendants, then waved a hand covered in rings towards the gatehouse and some garrison commander out of sight.

'Here we go,' Broudiccan muttered grimly as the gates creaked apart in a rattling of chains and a golden crack of light.

A block of half-masked soldiers encased in full plate armour of flawless gold and wielding wickedly curved polearms marched forth. A column with a rank of ten seamlessly became two columns with a rank of five, the marchers splitting to assume positions either side of the gate. A mighty *bang* reverberated about the Solar as two-hundred men of the Solar Guard smacked the butts of their weapons into the ground, turned forty-five degrees to left or right, and then stamped their boot to the flagstones.

The gryph-hound, Crow, lashed his tail.

Hamilcar rubbed the beast's heavy beak to soothe him. 'You heard the king.' He turned to Broudiccan and Thracius with a grin. 'He asked us to come in peace.'

The sealing of the gates actually brightened the gatehouse considerably. Natural light poured in through tall, outwards slanted windows, then burned like fire across the doors' gold and electrum panelling. The walls were that same pitiless white. Hamilcar grimaced and held up a hand as a woman in jewelled armour approached through the files of Solar Guard, bent light streaming from her armour's faceted edges in a dazzling spray of colours.

'I had expected to be welcomed by General Sarmiel el Talame,' he grunted. 'It was his legion that treated with us in the border deserts of the sankrit. He was the one who arranged this audience once we had explained your city's danger.'

The woman did not answer.

Everything about her spoke of remoteness, light without warmth.

Steeling himself with a deep breath, he turned to look directly at her.

Within her searing aura, he made out a smudge of darkness, skin, olive brown, and long dark hair ornamented with some kind of gold. Tears began to fill his eyes as he found the glittering lines of powdered gold drawn from the corners of the woman's eyes. One of the Rays of the sun-king. He gave her a pained grin.

Crow, he held by the scruff to settle his growls.

'The sun-king, Joraad el Ranoon, eternally glorious king of earth and sky, commands the surrender of your arms,' she said.

Hamilcar rubbed his eyes and frowned. Sarmiel had not prepared them for that.

In addition to her armour, the woman bore an emerald-hilted tulwar, though it was belted in a scabbard of jewelled silk and could only have been ceremonial in function. Hamilcar squinted to the guards. He had counted about fifty outside, but if there had been any more waiting inside he could not tell, and one gold-armoured figure blurred into another here. How they saw *him*, he couldn't fathom.

He supposed they got used to it.

'You don't draw the teeth from a bear and expect it to behave.'

Broudiccan snorted, and clutched his massive thunderaxe possessively.

'Weapons are not permitted in the presence of the sun-king,' the woman said.

'Perhaps we should oblige them in this,' Thracius counselled.

'Am I able to speak to el Ranoon directly through...?' Hamilcar waved vaguely over the blankly starring thrall. 'This? An evil you are ill prepared for rides before us. Trickery is his weapon. Even your great citadel cannot be counted a haven. We are here to defend your kingdom, to test the sharpness of the vampire's wits on Hamilcar's blade.'

The woman's eyelids fluttered, as if the host sought to wake but couldn't. 'The sun-king will settle for your blade, Lord-Castellant, if your followers will submit to having their weapons bound to the sheaths.'

Hamilcar conceded. He tossed his halberd to a barely visible Solar Guard and with a nod of assent bade Broudiccan stow his axe. The woman waved a gauntleted hand – the light in its path cut to daggered purples and greens – and called for silk for binding.

'Divine majesty.' A captain of the Solar Guard crouched to one knee as men moved amongst the glowering Astral Templars bearing bolts of silk, then bowed his head to the Ray as though he addressed his king in person. 'The crowds have been cleared from the Solar. My men have secured the plaza and the legions return the people to the city.'

'You have done well.' Her eyes rolled backwards for a spell, the attentions of the puppet-lord momentarily elsewhere, and then the dolorous clangour of gongs and horns sounded from the ramparts.

Hamilcar squinted towards the high windows. Treating with a sovereign power was one part fine words to nine parts theatre.

And Hamilcar Bear-Eater knew theatre.

'I was not advised on any further ceremony.'

The Ray nodded, as if to herself, then backed away. The pain in Hamilcar's eyes receded appreciably. A few paces back she drew her ornamental blade from its sheath. It was a beautiful thing, as if drawn whole from the heart of a star.

'The return of Sigmar and the elder pantheon has been awaited for centuries. Their disappearance was never explained to us.' She lowered her head, and raised her sword flat across her palms to be kissed by the light that poured through the windows. 'The people will not stand idle. Better they remain ignorant of what passes between us. I am the sun-king of Jercho, imposter, and Sigmar is dead to me.'

Hamilcar bellowed as the woman swung for him. He raised an arm. Sparks tore from the sword's curved blade and it slid down the angle of his vambrace. A twist, a shove, and he threw the mortal off. She spun once before she landed, light spearing from her as though a cut diamond had been flicked across the face of the sun, any idea of pursuit discouraged with burning pins to the eyes. With a grunt, Hamilcar pulled up. Pain turned his face behind the shade of his own pauldron, eyes narrowed to tear-filled slits.

Dull things in their glorious plate, the Solar Guard moved in.

There was a reluctance to their step, but they came anyway, a reminder of why Hamilcar had always despised biddable warriors, served up in gold.

Whatever orders they had been given it was clear they had been told to execute them quietly, for without a cry or an oath they drew back their polearms and charged. Hamilcar was not about to oblige them their desire for silence.

Say one thing for Hamilcar Bear-Eater: he was loud.

With a bellow that caused the panelling on the gates behind him to rattle and the imprisoned moon dragon of Jercho to shift in its chains, he backhanded an incoming polearm from his chest, then drove his elbow into its wielder's helmet with force enough to crack the man's skull against his spine. Thracius shattered another's breastplate with a punch that threw him into the wall. The Liberator Prime beat on his breastplate and roared. Disappointment had made him wrathful, and Hamilcar was almost glad that he did not have a weapon. With an inchoate beast-sound Thracius dragged a knight from his comrades by the point of his polearm, then dashed him against the ceiling.

Even unarmed, the Stormcasts were proving more than the elite warriors of Jercho had been prepared for.

With the courage of one who bore no share of danger, the Ray exhorted her faltering soldiers to press that attack. 'They are unarmed. Bring down one, just one, and the sun will shine forever on you all.' Her blade wove a dazzling pattern of sunsteel and diamond. It was a struggle just to look at her. Crow drew onto its haunches to leap for her, only for Hamilcar to throw his arm down across him like a barrier.

'Down.'

The woman laughed coldly. 'As the sun forever shines, so is Sigmar prideful.'

'I am not Sigmar. Though the resemblance is marked.'

The thrall leapt forwards. Hamilcar unclipped his warding lantern just as the woman came within reach. The heavy sigmarite shutters struck her a mighty blow across the jaw, and she hit the floor like a pouch of gemstones. Hamilcar walked towards her recumbent form, rubbing his eyes, as Broudiccan and Thracius saw to the last of the Solar Guards.

'Could Mannfred have worked his claws so deep so soon?' asked Broudiccan. The giant Decimator was on one knee, looking over his shoulder as he sat an unconscious knight against the wall.

'Mannfred would have known better. He would have sent more men.' Blinking quickly, he turned to the downed woman. 'Tell me why–'

Before he could finish, a knife appeared in the woman's hand. Hamilcar drew back, but then, eyes glassed by distance, she ran the knife across her own throat. A red line appeared, and the glaze in her eyes cleared as the controlling spirit chose that moment to forsake her body. Its parting gift was a few moments of horrified incomprehension as the woman spluttered and gagged and clawed at Hamilcar's boot as if he had the power to save her. And then she was still.

Hamilcar clicked his tongue.

He had died one time too many to be moved by barbarity now.

'Whatever the reason, the sun-king wants us dead.'

'Agreed,' said Thracius.

Broudiccan spat on the ground as he rose. 'And they say that Chaos never reached here.'

'Chaos doesn't always march with an army,' said Hamilcar. 'You can travel the seven realms to the farthest winterland and still find that Chaos got there first.'

'Then we remove its stain from our boot heel,' said Broudiccan, grimly.

'Agreed,' said Thracius.

Hamilcar and his brothers looked up to see Crow pacing restively before the electrum panelling of a heavy wooden door. The gryph-hound stared at Hamilcar. Intelligence and aggression in its eyes. Hamilcar grinned.

Retrieving his halberd, Hamilcar kicked the doors in. They smashed outwards and splintered against the walls of a corridor. Immediately, he recoiled. It was a blistering desert of pastel stone and points of gold without colour or finish, such was the unnatural intensity of light that blazed through its enormous windows. Despite the pain in his eyes, Hamilcar marvelled. No army could storm the sun-king's citadel and prevail. No agent or saboteur could make it this far and navigate any further undiscovered.

'Some ambassadors we turned out to be,' said Thracius, sorrowfully.

'Ambassadors.' Hamilcar gave a snort. 'Describe me thus again and I'll rinse your mouth with sand.'

Broudiccan adjusted the sit of his dented helm and regarded them both sourly.

'The sun-king seeks to thwart our great task and now he will pay for his crime. Such is the rule of Hamilcar!' Hamilcar turned to his men, lifting his voice, and holding his halberd high. 'We will bleed him, brothers. And give his kingdom to Sigmar!'

'To Sigmar!' they bellowed in return.

'*Hamilcar!*' he roared back at them, until the names were interchangeable.

His heart beat faster than the continuing medley of the sun-king's horns and gongs as Crow tore off down the corridor. Hamilcar powered after him, the ground-eating stride of a demigod, his warriors close behind. Joraad could be anywhere, but he would know exactly what was loose in his citadel. Through a door and the corridor became another, great open space, its windows washing it with molten gold. Hamilcar staggered, another blow to eyes that were still raw. There was a gargling cry from ahead, short-lived, then a slam of gryph-hound against metal, against stone wall. Hamilcar stepped over the savaged Solar Guard and into a staircase. It was marginally darker inside, luminous rather than blinding, dark enough to see provided one shared the sight with superimposed images of his eyeballs' veins.

The Astral Templars clattered down the stairs.

Hamilcar broke open another door.

It was some kind of receiving hall. A large wooden table was arrayed with nuts, dates and cured meats, presented as artworks on golden platters. Sunlight fell through slanted windows like taffeta ribbons, along with a natural breeze. A marble statue of womanly splendour poured water into a font from a horn of plenty. The cool chuckle of running water was a delight, so unexpected that Hamilcar almost charged right through the door and into the table.

The spread teetered on its platters.

His stomach stirred in sudden interest.

The Sea of Bones had been a journey to tax even the limitless constitution of the Stormcast Eternals and he had taken little but water and salted sankrit since. With an act of will that impressed even himself he ignored the growls of his stomach to focus on those of Crow, and the pound of armoured footsteps approaching from the other door across from the far end of the table.

'Judicators, left and right.'

With exaggerated cutting gestures of his hand he directed the Judicators to either side of the long table, then leapt onto it two-footed. The elaborate vittle sculptures descended to the floor with a crash. He kicked aside a pyramid of dates that had somehow remained standing and twirled his halberd. The Judicators' boltstorm crossbows sparked and whined as bolts of azyrite energy materialised in their tracks, fizzing against aetheric strings that were suddenly taut.

'Loose on my order,' Hamilcar bellowed, for there was no warrior who could not be improved by heeding the example of Hamilcar. 'I claim the city of Jercho for Sigmar. The fewer of its people I have to kill, the greater will be his prize.'

With a crashing of gold-barred timbers, a phalanx of leather and bronze-clad common soldiery fell through the far door. 'Hold!' roared Hamilcar, and the mortal legionaries checked back in disarray at the monstrous visage he must have presented.

Pushing and cussing, a slightly bent old man draped in black silks with light silver vambraces and coif forced his way up from the rear ranks. 'Is this the same legion that crushed the sankrit at Heliopalis, first through the breach at Anatoly? If I didn't know better, then I–' The newcomer hesitated as he saw Hamilcar up on the dining table. Without tearing his eyes away, he too gestured his men to stand down. With clear relief, they did so. 'Lord-Castellant,' he said.

Hamilcar might have laughed. He hadn't even been as pleased to see the man when he'd first stumbled into him, blind with thirst, lost and half-mad from a sun that never set.

'Sarmiel! Praise whoever you like for you!'

The Jerchese general did not return Hamilcar's welcome. 'There were reports of fighting in the gatehouse.'

A shrug. 'That was us.'

'I vouched for you before the sun-king himself. Do you know what that means? A dozen Solar Guard are dead!'

'At least twice as many still live. Is that the work of invaders?'

Sarmiel hesitated at that, Hamilcar saw. He already doubted the truth of his reports or he would have come in fighting and to hell with explanations.

That was all the opening Hamilcar needed.

He had mastered his rhetoric in debate with the God-King himself, the Sigmarabulum crowded to its rafters by the admiring folk of Azyr, there to witness a bout between champions. They were a dozen spear-lengths apart, Hamilcar and the mortal man, but he lowered his halberd and extended a hand in friendship.

'You remember the day we met. You remember what you said to me? I know you do because you had to tell me again after you had given me water and I became sensible.'

A nod. 'That to have crossed the Sea of Bones you could only have been sent by Sigmar.'

'You had me at your mercy. Now I have you at mine.'

His halberd tinked as its blade touched the flagstones.

Sarmiel appeared to sag in surrender. No sooner had he done so, however, than the stoop he had been carrying seemed to evaporate off him. He sheathed his sword with a shake of the head. 'I doubt I could stop you anyway. Not with this lot.' A glare at his men.

'I didn't want to be the one to say it.' Hamilcar grinned.

'I knew something was amiss when el Ranoon removed me

DAVID GUYMER

from your honour guard. No. Before then. Since he moved his court to the Moon Palace.'

'Moon Palace?'

'It is where the first sun-king imprisoned the night.'

Hamilcar and Broudiccan shared a look.

'Take us there.'

Hamilcar did not even realise he had been asleep.

He gasped, fighting with nothing, arms bulging as he fought to drive the... *something* from his breastplate. There was a pain in his heart. Black iron cracked his ribs like the shell of a nut and dug for the soft beating pulp within. With a roar he lashed out, his halberd having somehow found its way into his hand, and clove at the Abyssal's neck. The splitting of stone and the crack as it hit the ground broke the dream logic, and he blinked the bloody image of his murderer, Ashigorath, back into nightmare.

In its place came the prattling of a fountain, the click and chirrup of insects, the rustle of leaves. Moonlit petals crept over the ledges of windows that faced in from no part of the fortress that Hamilcar could remember seeing. He held his chest and drew a deep breath. The air was jasmine-scented, as cool as dead iron. He looked back to the steel-barred portal that el Talame's key had seen them past.

'Here is where the night is bound,' said the old general. 'And everything that goes with it.'

'Fitting,' Hamilcar grunted.

Broudiccan and the others said nothing. Hamilcar knew no fear. They knew better than to doubt it.

The fountain he had heard was a few score yards from the portal, in a column of moonlight that the trees seemed to have twisted themselves to avoid. He walked to the basin. Kneeling, he splashed cool water into his face. As the ripples cleared, he saw himself looking into a face that he almost recognised: the tawny beard, scuffed by serried lines of scars, the thorny branch tattoo that swirled around his eye.

The eye however, he avoided looking into too deeply.

Say one thing for Hamilcar Bear-Eater: he wasn't perfect. He dashed the reflection with his gauntlet.

Memories of death and reforging had never before troubled him while he had been awake. Was he awake in this place? He wondered, briefly, if el Talame ever slept and if he did, if he dreamed.

Crow whined up at him as he rubbed his breastplate.

Sigmar, would the dreams never leave him?

He turned to el Talame. 'The sun-king. Point me at him.'

The general pointed through a crumbling stone arch. He was afraid to be here, but he marshalled it well, achieving as much as Hamilcar with far less in his making. Determined to be the champion of a god that warriors would kneel to, he shrugged the ache aside, then rose, flicking dream water from his fingers, and ducked under the arch.

The fact that they moved through the heart of the citadel of Jercho, or some timeless, dreamscaped version of it, was artfully masked by weeping orchids and clambering vines. Night birds twittered in backwards verse and things both ageless and unseen scampered amongst the branches. Blossoms drifted on the air as they need never fall.

Broudiccan tramped after him, grim, solid.

'Do you think this place would resist a Chaos invasion if it came?' Hamilcar asked him, surprised at how the garden's solemnity made him whisper.

'No. If an army can breach the Sea of Bones then Jercho and her sisters will fall.'

They passed onto a bridge over a gurgling stream, causing the wood to creak under the weight of their armour.

'It needn't be an army,' said Hamilcar. 'Mannfred can build an army. I saw it myself in Cartha–'

'–hold!'

Broudiccan caught his shoulder and the column of Astral Templars and Jercho legionaries clattered to a halt.

The space beyond the bridge was littered with small stone benches and statues that had been subjected to centuries of weathering and then shrouded in creepers. The moonlight that filtered through the ornamental trees gleamed where it touched bare stone and cut sharply across reflective pools and small bowls of water. A young man with the entitled impatience of a nobleman rested with one arm against a statue, as though awaiting an audience. He was lightly armoured in a fitted leather lorica with gold accoutrements and a silk cloak swept over one shoulder. A fine pair of steel swords with jewelled hilts were scabbarded at his belt, and rested against the statue beside him was a long spear with a jade-coloured pennant tied around the base of the blade. Seeing Hamilcar at the same time as Hamilcar saw him, he swept up his spear and sauntered towards them.

Broudiccan didn't wait for any sign of malice.

Striding towards the noble he planted his boot heel through the man's chest, strength that had been beaten into him on the God-King's anvil lifting the mortal from his feet and smashing him back against the statue. The youth dropped in a clatter of lorica scales into a reflective pool, broken, Hamilcar would have thought, but then he vaulted agilely to his feet. He hissed, bleeding from his mouth. His spear began to hum as he spun it.

And something that no man should possess glittered in the moonlight.

Fangs.

'By the gods, that's Gilgazed,' el Talame stuttered, agog, pointing with his tulwar, 'el Raniel's eldest son.'

Snake-quick, the vampire struck Broudiccan like a spear thrown at a wall. The Decimator's enormous axe whirled as fast as the vampire's spear could match. Blade struck blade, haft against haft; claps of thunder shook invisible birds from their roosts amongst the trees as storm-fused barbarian battled undying fiend.

Hamilcar turned from his brother's fight, the splash of water warning of the arrival of others from downstream. The vampire's speed made him little more than a blur, a sweeping depression in the surface of the water that raced towards Hamilcar at the foot of the bridge.

The vampire's blade came at him like the lance head of a galloping knight, hard enough and fast enough in that first dramatic instant of arrival to have speared through dragon scale had Hamilcar not had the wherewithal to duck. It sliced across him. Using his momentum to turn, Hamilcar backhanded the rising butt of his halberd across the vampire's jaw. The knight's face snapped back and spun away. Hamilcar forced the rest of the vampire's body to follow. A boot to the back bent the vampire over the bridge's handrail. Hamilcar lent in, drew his gladius, and rammed the stabbing blade through the vampire's spine. The fiend's legs turned to jelly, and Hamilcar's boot held him where he was. Boot transferred to knee and then he leant in to bite down on the vampire's ear. His teeth tore through cartilage, his mouth filled sluggishly with brackish warm blood, and then he put his full strength through his knee.

The handrail broke with a splintering crack and the howling vampire dropped the short way to the water. Hamilcar spat his bloody ear after him and roared.

He was Hamilcar of the Astral Templars. Eater of Bears. Sigmar would look upon him and then turn to his own two hands to marvel at the titan they had wrought.

The vampire writhed in the shallow water, and the slower men in clanking golden plate that had been hurrying to the bridge from the same direction looked up in surprise. Hamilcar grinned at them. 'Hamilcaaar!' He leapt, two-footed, and flattened the two men into the rocky streambed where the first still scrabbled madly to claw his way out. These were not vampires; they were mortal.

They never stood a chance.

'Slaughter the infidels!' cried a voice, cultured, but too steeped in the intonations of the Jerchese to be anything but a native. 'By order of the sun-king!'

With a roar, four-score Solar Guards surged up the paths that converged on the little bridge and its island folly. A bolt-storm bolt blasted a knight to scraps of liquid gold and cast the two behind into the trees with the aftershock. Prosecutors took wing. While Hamilcar and Broudiccan had fought, Thracius and el Talame had organised their men and they moved to oppose their attackers now. Armed and ready, Hamilcar would have counted on his dozen alone against five times the number of mortal warriors that assaulted them now, but for every ten heavy knights there was a sneering nobleman with an exotic blade and fangs.

With a hiss of fury, a vampire in oiled green lorica scales broke from his unit of mortals and punched through a line of el Talame's soldiers like a ballista bolt fired from Shyish. Hamilcar yelled for Thracius as men began to cartwheel from the frenzied vampire.

Before the Liberator-Prime could intervene, the bushes behind the vampire burst apart and Crow bore the undying champion to the ground. There was a gargling scream as the gryph-hound's beak tore through the armour of its chest. Hamilcar grunted at the sudden, shared pain in his breast, and splashed for the stream's bank. Inexplicably breathless, he turned to see Broudiccan. The Decimator was now holding his own against three more, warring through the rubble of demolished statuary.

The Stormcast could handle the vampires, Hamilcar had no doubt, but that still left the Solar Guards.

'Hold them, Thracius!' he bellowed. He turned to find el Talame, shouting instructions to his own men, beset, on the other side of the bridge. Their rear ranks were ankle-deep in the water. 'With me, my friend. Bring me to the sun-king.'

'Take your own,' the general called back across the water. 'They will be more use to you.'

'The Bear-Eaters can hold their own. You cannot. And I would hate to come so far to strike the wrong head from its shoulders.' His chest was tight. Breathing came hard. 'Lead me through this nightmare!'

One of Thracius' Liberators took the slack as el Talame and his soldiers splashed across the water to Hamilcar's side. The general himself was last, covered by a boltstorm from a kneeling Judicator that drove the Solar Guard from the water's edge and allowed the Liberator to put down the vampire that had led them. Another with a snarling leopard daubed across his facemask took station on the bridge and grimly stood their ground.

'This way.' El Talame swept past Hamilcar. The pace he set was impressive for one so old, but Hamilcar had time enough to look back and see Broudiccan's thunderaxe obliterate a statue and shred a dozen Solar Guard with shrapnel and still better it. He swatted aside a silver bower that grew across the path.

Unkempt for a court. And Hamilcar had once ruled from a cave.

And just like that he began to laugh.

Mortality had never seemed so distant.

With strength and vigour twenty times a mortal man's, he forged a path to the front of the company of warriors, and forced his way through a tangle of ornamental dwarf trees to stumble into a clearing.

An elevated platform of eerie silver-grey stone rose above the small trees and tiered gardens. It looked ancient. The moon shone with a caged, furious splendour, shackled to the form of a splintered throne in which sat the sun-king, Joraad el Ranoon.

His golden mask beheld Hamilcar from his high throne.

With a series of shouts intended to bolster each other's courage, el Talame's men took the steps. In response the sun-king lifted one sleeve from the shining rest of his throne.

At his gesture a host of men and women, and even children, shuffled, unseeing, from the crackling glare of the throne and moved to block the steps. Some wore blazing suits of armour, similar to the woman that Hamilcar had bested in the gatehouse, although nothing so impressive in this penumbral shadow-realm. Others were in simple habits emblazoned with the unsetting sun. None of them spoke, smiled, or even looked down at the cracked steps as they pressed together between the oncoming soldiers and their king. If there was one amongst them that could appreciate the incongruity of that emblem in this place then it was the self-proclaimed god-king on the throne behind them, but he did not seem to.

The soldiers hesitated a few steps below the vacant Rays.

The Rays themselves looked over the soldiers as if they were blind, and soporific with the experience of their remaining senses.

'You seek to best me with children,' Hamilcar shouted up to the impassive sun-king. 'Know that you face Hamilcar of the Astral Templars. I am a Stormcast Eternal!' Hamilcar hefted his halberd high above his head, his lantern in the other. 'Tell the Lord of Death when you cross the Stygxx Gate that it is the Bear-Eater that sends you, prince of lies. Tell him that you are down payment on the soul of a brother.'

The assembled host opened their mouths, and with one voice alone they spoke.

'The men you have killed thus far have followed me freely. Not by choice perhaps, but they could have chosen death and that is as much a choice as any other. But these,' the enthroned king waved a hand over his thralls. The proximity to his person of genuine peril must have caused his attention to lapse somewhat, for several of the thralls mimicked the gesture. 'These are innocents. You will have to butcher them all to reach me, *Eternal*. I will see to it. Has Sigmar forged you the stomach for it?'

Joraad leaned forward then, and in a hundred distinct voices, male and female, old and young, began to laugh.

With a grunt, Hamilcar tossed up his halberd, reversed the grip, and then hurled it.

Like a javelin it hissed from his extended arm over the heads of the uncaring slaves and through el Ranoon's belly.

There was a snarl of moonlight as the blade tip skewered him to his throne's high back. A cry tore from Joraad's throat. Blood and dark lumpy juices spurted from the hole made by the halberd shaft and turned the king's banyan silks black. The gathered Rays echoed their master's scream, then one-by-one passed into unconscious. The sheer number of them packed onto the steps kept them from falling far.

'They call me the Bear-Eater,' he called up to the pitifully crying sun-king. 'You do not want to test my stomach.'

He frowned then as the increasingly pale king of Jercho slumped forward onto the halberd shaft.

'Light above,' muttered el Talame. 'Is it dead?'

'He is.' Hamilcar was surprised.

Joraad el Ranoon was no vampire. It was true then: anyone could make a mistake.

Perhaps the mind-controlling magicks by which he ruled would have been affected by the transition to unlife. Or perhaps the land of the unsetting sun was simply no place for a vampire king.

'I suspect Mannfred found him more useful as a willing puppet than a slave.'

'So your vampire is still out there?'

Hamilcar laughed aloud at that, despite his disappointment at seeing the betrayer slip through his fingers once again. There was truth in what the old man said.

The vampire was his.

'There is only so much of Ghur for him to run into. Say one thing for Hamilcar – in the end, he always triumphs.'

Pantheon

Guy Haley

There was a lantern in the skies over Azyr – shining Sigendil, the High Star of Azyr, beacon of Sigmaron. Surrounding its body was a mechanism of great art, a thing of sliding spheres pierced with fretwork. With the shifting of the immense clockwork Sigendil twinkled, and shone the brightest of all the stars in the heavens of the Celestial Realm.

The inhabitants of Azyr loved it well. Sailors charted safe courses across stormy seas by its light. Mothers hushed crying children and pointed, saying, 'There is the holy light of our God-King, see how he watches over you as you sleep.' Merchants swore oaths by it and laws were ratified by its light, so constant it was, for Sigendil never moved from its appointed place in the sky as other stars did. In an age of awful wonder, the matchless light of Sigendil was a source of certainty.

But though it was itself invarying, Sigendil had witnessed change, even in Azyr.

Far to the north towered Mount Celestian, Azyr's greatest peak. Only once in history had the mountain been assailed, when Sigmar's great hammer Ghal Maraz smashed its peak away, leaving a lofty plateau dominated by a lake of shining blue. Upon its shores he built a city whose scale and glory outshone even Azyrheim, for it was made to be the abode of gods, not mortals. The divine survivors of the World-That-Was gathered under Sigmar's banner on Celestian, to rule the Eight Mortal Realms.

There was a castle of bones so huge one would think them carved fancily, though any who touched them would find them dry and osseous. Another dwelling was a wooden stockade, much splintered and strewn about with more bones, these gnawed upon. To the east were twin, squat fortresses, one of iron and one of frozen fire. To the west was a trio of slender towers whose forms, though similar, reflected the differing temperaments of their builders. In a vale of scented woods where the waters of Lake Celestian tumbled to the lands below, grew an oak of inconceivable size.

At the centre of the city temples gathered upon a vast silver acropolis. From their midst a tower of blue light pierced Azyr's busy skies. Atop it was situated the Court of the Gods, a colonnaded space from whose vantage all the Mortal Realms could be seen. Thrones fit for titans ringed it – bone for Nagash, white marble for Tyrion, silver for Teclis, dark stone for Malerion, fire-hued amber for Grimnir and rustless steel for his brother, Grungni. Alarielle's was of pale heartwood rooted in the stone, while Sigmar's own gleamed golden. The thrones looked inward to the legendary Mirror of Bayla, a gleaming sheet of silver four yards across.

Together, mountain, city and court were known as the Highheim, the parliament of the gods in more peaceful ages.

No longer. The court had stood deserted for aeons.

The Ages of Myth had passed thousands of years ago. Mortals had forgotten the Highheim. Silence lay upon the city as thickly as the spent stardust that drifted in its thoroughfares.

That day, life returned a while. A lone figure trod the court. Noble of aspect and mightier than the greatest mortal, he was dwarfed by the buildings, and so his own stature was uncertain. He looked like the man he had been, ages gone in a different world. But god he was – Sigmar, the architect and lord of the city, and uniter of the gods.

Sigmar stood between the columns. Overhead the spectacular heavens of Azyr turned, to the south blazed matchless Sigendil, almost but not quite obscuring the husk of the World-That-Was behind it. Scented wind teased out Sigmar's long golden hair and stirred his cloak.

He waited impatiently. Though a god, he had a man's humours still. His patience had been exhausted by the long vigil of the Age of Chaos. Now his war was in motion, Sigmar had ceased to plan. He wanted to act.

Yet he must wait.

Night did its complex dance, the wheeling stars a backcloth to the motions of zodiacal beasts and divine mechanisms that sailed the lower heavens. Dawn arrived to find Sigmar deep in thought, head bent over the Mirror of Bayla. Would she come? He did not truly know. Their friendship had passed with the elder days.

The first rays of the sun struck the white pediment of the colonnade, washing marble orange. Sigmar's head rose. Sensing magic, he stood.

A glow took hold around the throne of Alarielle. The ancient wood creaked and groaned. It emitted a screeching crack, so that Sigmar thought it might explode, but it shuddered, and from its tall back fresh shoots sprouted, growing unnaturally fast, leaves budding from them as they unfurled and reached skyward. The throne's roots flexed, cracking the paving, the slow might of trees quickened by divine power.

There was a wink of light, then another, and another still, until a cloud of golden motes danced around like fireflies. The swarm thickened and coalesced, becoming the form of a tall, proud woman. The scent of rising sap and luxuriant flowers wafted over the god king. The lights solidified, until the features of Alarielle could be clearly discerned. Light faded. The throne put out a crown of fragrant blossom, framing the goddess' broad wings of leaf and wood in white flowers.

Alarielle wore a crescent helm-crown, and carried a sinuous glaive. Her pale green skin was like that of a beautiful mortal's, save her right hand, which was of strong, clawed branches.

Sigmar broke into a smile. 'Alarielle, the lady of life. You came.'

Alarielle walked toward him, the motes of magic that made her image breaking apart a little as she moved. Her presence made the mirror shine. 'I can spare you this projection, Sigmar of the tribes of men, for a short while. Speak and tell me why you called me back to this place.'

'I thank you for coming. I appreciate the effort you have put forth.'

'You do right in thanking me.' Where she trod, delicate flowers sprang from the cracks in the paving. 'The days when you might summon me are no more, prince.' Her pupilless green eyes flashed in challenge.

Sigmar bowed. 'I would not dream of summoning you. I invited, you responded. It is so good to see you again.'

A small smile curved Alarielle's lips. 'So the mighty Sigmar has learned humility. I had thought to find you more arrogant than ever. Your armies march across all the Mortal Realms. To unleash war on the four lords of Chaos alone is not the act of a humble man. Your rashness almost ended me, you realise.'

'For that, my lady, you have my eternal apologies.'

She walked past him, trailing the smell of growth and new

life, and looked out over the Highheim's deserted ways. 'No matter. Your actions, though impetuous, led to my rebirth and reinvigoration. You reawakened me. I spent too long brooding on defeat. If you had not caused my death, I would have been destroyed.' She swept her gaze across the empty city. 'So much beauty here, but it is sterile, bereft of life and purpose. It saddens me,' she said. She looked at him. 'I believed in your vision once, but it failed. If you have come to ask me to rejoin you here, to reform the pantheon of old, I will not.'

'I did not ask you here to reform our old order,' he said. 'Perhaps one day, but not now.'

'Perhaps then I will be interested, when a new season comes upon me,' she shrugged. 'Perhaps not.' She sighed, the air she exhaled dancing with colourful insects. 'If you ask for alliance, you already have it. My warriors fight alongside yours. Any reluctance the wargroves felt toward your warriors of lightning is fading. War is joined on all fronts.'

'I thank you for that also,' he said, 'and my Stormcast Eternals will aid the people of the forests wherever they may be found. But asking for alliance is also not my intent.'

'Then what do you want from me?' she asked, curious.

'Something more subtle than blades,' he said. 'Come with me.' He reached to take her hand. His fingers passed through the glowing lights making up her form, but she followed when he walked to the flat silver of the Mirror of Bayla.

'The gift of the Mage Bayla to the pantheon of old,' he said.

'I remember,' she said. 'Its use allows the viewer to see whither he will, be it in any realm.'

'That is so,' he said. He passed a hand over the metal. 'It is into the past that we shall look, into another time and place. We will witness the quest of Sanasay Bayla himself.'

'Are we to see the forging of this artefact?' she asked.

Sigmar smiled. 'We shall look back further than that, to the time he was a sage and a seeker in Andamar, at the far edges of Ghyran.'

'A seeker after what?' asked Alarielle. Her concern was rarely with thinking creatures of flesh. Her domain was of plants and growing things, and the wild spaces of the worlds. She knew little more of Bayla than she did of other short-lived fleshlings.

The mirror filled with swirling cloud. Lights flashed in the vapour, steadying until an image could be seen: a handsome man with walnut brown skin and a ready smile. Intelligence flashed in his eyes, and a hunger.

'He sought what all mortals seek,' Sigmar said. 'Knowledge.'

The image clarified, and the two gods looked back far in to the past, to a time before the coming of Chaos.

There came a day when the Mage Sanasay Bayla had learned all he could from the great minds of his era. After long study he was acclaimed as the finest thinker of his generation, and the most powerful wizard in all of Ghyran. His family rejoiced in his achievements, but for him it was not enough. Sanasay Bayla lacked purpose, and it troubled him.

He lay in bed, staring through the glassless windows at dancing green auroras over the south. In Andamar, Ghyran's life ran even into the sky.

Bayla exhaled loudly, waking his wife.

'What are you sighing about there, Sanasay?' she said sleepily.

'I do not mean to wake you,' he said.

'You did.' She smiled and rested her hand on his chest. 'What troubles you, my love?'

He was silent, and so his wife poked him.

'You lay hands on the greatest mage in Andamar, if not all of Ghyran?' he asked in mock outrage.

She laughed, a sound that meant the most to him in all the world. 'Tell me. If the greatest mage in Andamar, if not all of Ghyran, cannot confide in his wife, then he is a poor man, though a great wizard.'

Bayla frowned and laced his fingers behind his head. 'I have unlocked many of the mysteries of the world,' he said. 'I have mastered five of the eight schools of pure magic. I understand the rest well enough, and know sufficient of the darker arts to leave them alone. Every question I ask, I find the answer to. I am bored, my wife. I must set myself a challenge that will test me. I need a purpose. I need to know why I do what I do, and to what end I should put my great knowledge."

'You could try getting up early every day, organising the household, seeing the children are cared for and that our finances do not collapse while you are riddling with fell beings,' she said. 'There is purpose there.'

He harrumphed.

'I am teasing you, my love.' She yawned.

'I am without goal or cause. I must find out what it is I want,' he said. 'Then I shall be satisfied.'

'What of the Realms' End? You have never been there. It is said all knowledge can be learned where the realms cease to be.'

'A myth,' he said. 'I determined long ago that it does not exist. The Realms are vast, perhaps infinite. I have travelled far, but never seen it. Every text I read suggests it is only a story.'

'Then be content with what you have, my darling.'

'Although I have much, the concern dogs me that there is more, if I but knew what to look for,' he said worriedly. 'I risk missing my greatest achievement.'

'Surely the gods could help,' she said. 'Why don't you ask them?'

She fell asleep. Sanasay Bayla could not. A new idea had come to him complete, and he set about planning its execution.

His wife probably meant for him to go to the temples, and consult with the priests there. But Sanasay was not like other men.

In Andamar's Temple of Teclis the Wise, there was a tower of marble so slender only one person could climb the winding stair. As the stair neared the peak, it grew so narrow that the climber must proceed sideways. Finally, it opened via a thin hole onto a platform big enough for a single person to sit. On every side was a dizzying drop. The tiniest slip would condemn a man to a long fall and a swift death. Sanasay could have cast a spell upon himself, or used one of his marvellous devices, or conjured a great beast to fly to the top of the tower, but the gods dislike those that cheat.

He crept onto the pinnacle. Wind tugged at him as he unwrapped his mat and laid it on the moist stone, careful not to drop the sacred objects rolled within. When they were laid out in the proper manner, he sat cross-legged in the middle of the pinnacle. He poured a single drop of mona nectar into a silver cup, whispering the necessary incantations, and drank it back. The bitter liquid made his tongue burn, but the sensation quickly passed, and his mind buzzed as it moved to a different plane.

Sanasay Bayla slipped into a deep trance.

When he opened his eyes, he was walking upon clouds in a world with five suns. A nearer radiance turned the clouds to gold, forcing his eyes into slits. When he opened them, there was a tall figure not far ahead, made from purest light. His features were similar to man but he was not of his race. His garb was outlandish.

'Great Teclis!' called Bayla, and fell to his knees on the clouds.

'Sanasay Bayla,' said Teclis. 'The quester after knowledge. You are brave to seek out the gods. I and my brother have watched you with much interest."

'Great Teclis,' said Bayla, 'who is the god of wisdom and arcane secrets. I beseech you, in all my–'

'Hush now, Bayla,' said Teclis in amusement. 'I know why you look for me. You wish to know if Realms' End is real, and how you might get there if it is.'

Bayla was not surprised the god could see into his thoughts. Teclis was the greatest wielder of magic in all the Realms.

'You have this hunted for this place before, but gave up,' said Teclis.

'I convinced myself it did not exist. Foolishly, perhaps.'

'I admire your dedication to your art, Sanasay Bayla,' said the god. 'I have known only a handful of your species able to learn so much of the ways of magic. But let it be known to you – too much knowledge is dangerous.'

'You warn the forewarned,' said Sanasay humbly.

'I will tell you, for your motives are pure and your achievements many. Realms' End exists.'

Bayla felt an uplifting in his heart. 'How can I go there?'

'There is a gate in the circling mountains that bound your land, those that no man has crossed. The gate leads into a tunnel that takes a route not of this plane. On the far side, Realms' End is to be found.'

'I will set out immediately!' said Bayla.

'There are two things you must know. The gate is locked, and there is no key. Only he who can forge the unforgeable can furnish you with one. On the far side is a monster which only death can kill. Find a way to overcome these obstacles, and Realms' End will be open to you.'

'I thank you, my lord,' said Bayla gratefully.

'Sanasay,' said Teclis. 'Be warned. This quest will consume you. You will discover your heart's desire, but you may not like what you find. Perhaps it would be best for you to remain at home.'

'I cannot know what it is until I see it,' said Bayla sadly. 'Though the risk is great, I must witness it for myself.'

'Then go with my blessing,' said Teclis. There was a clap of thunder. Bayla fell through the clouds. He landed hard in his meditating body. It rocked dangerously as he awoke, but he did not fall.

So it was he set out on his next task.

His wife pleaded with him not to go. The Iron Temples of the duardin were many years of travel away, and there was no guarantee its guardians would allow him within the precincts.

'I must!' he said. His young children clustered around their mother, and clutched at her skirts, but he was blinded by anguish, and could not see their tears. 'What if I turn away, and never realised my full potential?'

For six years he travelled, through many realmgates and over hundreds of lands. Finally, older, scarred and weary, he came to the Iron Temples in Chamon's Ferron Vale.

'You cannot enter,' said the temple guard, when Bayla had stated his case. 'This is sacred ground, dedicated to Grungni. No manling may go within.' So the conversation began, and so it continued, developing into bargaining, then arguing, but the duardin remained unmoved, and they would not let him inside.

Bayla went high into the mountains, where he could overlook the carved peaks and smoking forges of the Iron Temples. Powerful runes glowed in the rock and metal of its walls. For all his sorcerous ability, the wards of the temple were forever denied.

Miserable, Bayla descended the mountains into forests of iron-thorned trees. By a wall of rock aglitter with veins of ore, he made his camp and settled down for a night of brooding, staring into the flames of his campfire.

'Won't let you in, lad?' said a gruff voice.

Bayla started. Without his noticing, a duardin had taken a seat on the far side of the fire. His face was hooded, but from the shadows protruded a white beard of impressive length, and he smoked a pipe of bone so ancient it was polished smooth and stained dark with use. Bayla knew enough of Grungni's folk to recognise an elder when he saw one.

The stranger chuckled at Bayla's reaction. 'Sorry, lad, I have a habit of creeping up on people. My apologies. Do you mind if you share your fire?'

'Of course you may,' said Bayla, who was wise to the ways of strange encounters. 'Please, sit. I have a small measure of ale and food that I would gladly share.'

'Well!' the duardin said in appreciation. 'Hospitality like that in the wilds, eh? Very good, very, very good.'

Bayla handed over his ale skin, which the duardin drained to the last drop, and gave over his food, which the duardin shared generously. They ate in companionable silence. When they were done, the duardin sniffed deeply. 'Not bad. Tasty. I long for a crumb of chuf, but they don't make that in this time and place.' He fell silent a space and twiddled with his pipe, lost in his memories. 'So then,' he said brightly. 'What's a manling like you want with the smith god of my people?'

'I seek a key to the door in the mountains that will lead me to Realms' End,' Bayla said. He blinked in surprise. He had not intended to reveal his purpose, but there were the words, tripping off his tongue!

'Ahhh, well, Grungni can be a prickly sort. I have known

him for, well,' the duardin laughed again, a sound like rough stones being rasped together, 'a very long time. Tell you what, why don't you borrow mine?'

The duardin reached into his dirty jerkin and pulled out a slender key with five pointed teeth, three on top, two on the bottom, upon a leather thong. His massive fingers should never have been so deft, but he undid the tiny knot in the necklace easily and tossed the key across the fire. Bayla caught it in surprise.

'There you are, lad.'

'Is it real?' Bayla asked in amazement. 'I was told there was no key in all existence!'

'An aelf tell you that, did he?' said the dwarf sourly. 'Don't trust them. Besides,' he added slyly, 'he never said anything about outside existence, did he?'

'Thank you,' Bayla said.

'A fair bargain for your kindness, and that ale.' The dwarf stood up and brushed off his knees. 'Right then, got to be going. Things to do, people to sneak up on unawares.' He laughed at his own jest.

'Who are you?' asked Bayla.

Deep in the stranger's hood, eyes twinkled. 'Just a traveller, lad, much like yourself.' With that, he went into the night, and disappeared.

Bayla could not know if the key was genuine or not, but he had no choice. By the same tortuous route, the mage returned to Ghyran. The road to the mountains took him far from his home, but he was eager to complete his quest.

For a further three years he searched for the gate. Only by questioning the local inhabitants carefully did he glean an inkling as to its whereabouts, and even then he wasted many months in fruitless search. Strange lights shone on the far side of the mountains that no mortal had ever crossed, tantalising him unbearably.

Eventually, by chance it seemed, he came across a door barely big enough to admit him, set high in a cliff face. With trembling hands, Bayla slid the key home. It fit perfectly and turned smoothly, as if recently oiled. The door swung inward, and Bayla squeezed inside. At first he had to wriggle his way down a tiny tunnel, but it soon opened up into a wide, well-made passageway, with walls of fine masonry. By his magic he lit his way. Soon after his entrance, Bayla's ears were troubled by a thundering rumble, and a hot wind that went in and out – the breath of the monster that guarded the way. Several days of travel later, during which Bayla lived off bitter mosses and water dribbling down the walls, the tunnel opened up into a giant cave. At the centre was chained a wolf of impossible size. Its head was as large as a cathedral, and rested on paws big as houses. Four thick chains ran from its collar, securing it to anchors set in the wall. All through Bayla's walk the noise of its breathing had become louder. In the cave it howled like a hurricane. It looked asleep, but as he approached, eyes big as pools opened and stared redly at him.

'You cannot pass,' it said. 'None can, whether god or mortal. It is the law, of which I am prisoner and guardian both.'

'Then I shall kill you,' said Bayla.

The wolf gave out a howling laugh that buffeted the mage back and forth.

'You can try.'

Bayla had come prepared with every spell of death he could muster. Raising his arms, he flung back his head, and called down the most potent slaughter-curse in the realms.

The magic released was primordial and deadly. It screamed

as Bayla drew it from the rock of the mountain and fashioned it into a spear of crackling power. With a roaring incantation, he cast the energy at the wolf.

The magic hurtled at the beast, piercing it between the eyes. The wolf cocked its eyebrow, unharmed. 'You will have to do better than that,' it said.

Sanasay Bayla tried. Nothing worked. The wolf was impervious to the direst magics known. Frustrated, Bayla even attempted to stab it in its massive paw with his dagger. The metal shattered. The wolf grumbled with mirth.

'I have not had such entertainment in many ages,' it said.

Bayla glared at it. 'Let me pass,' he said.

'I shall not,' said the wolf.

'Then you leave me no choice.' Bayla pulled out a crystal phial, full of a dark liquid. Defiantly looking the wolf in the eye, Bayla threw down the stopper and drained the bottle. 'Poison,' Bayla said. 'Now we shall see who has the last laugh.'

He fell down, dead.

The world changed. Bayla's soul rose from his body. From rocks that now glowed with inner light rose screaming ghosts, luminous scythes in their hands. They rushed at him, fleshless jaws wide, swinging their weapons for the thread that joined Bayla's body to his soul.

Bayla had no intention to die completely. As the cavern receded from him at tremendous speed, he fought against the gatherers of souls with his magic, keeping them from severing his connection to the Mortal Realms. Through planes inhabited by the strangest things they sped, thundering down through veils of layered realities toward the Realm of Shyish, where the abode of mortals abut those places beyond even the gods' ken.

Bayla burst through a cavern roof, the gatherers swooping

around him. Shyish revealed its dreary landscapes. He flew over shadowy villages and moonlit meres, vast bone deserts and forests of trees that shivered with the sorrow of imprisoned souls. Parts of this land were roofed in stone, and from holes gnawed through it tumbled an endless rain of corpses, the dead of many realms come to take their final rest.

Ahead there was a mighty necropolis, a city of pyramids and bone towers whose edges crackled with a nimbus of soul light. The gatherers redoubled their attacks, their wails draining the warmth from Bayla's being, their scythes only ever a moment from reaping his soul.

The battle continued right to the gates in the city's wall of bone. Bayla halted. A man stood there, cadaverous, but alive. With a flick of his wrist he dismissed the gatherers of souls, leaving the disembodied essence of Bayla alone.

'You are dead, and yet your thread is not cut,' said the necromancer. 'Why do you resist the inevitable?'

'I am Sanasay Bayla, of Ghyran. I die because I wish to speak with the Lord of Death.'

The necromancer smiled, exposing black teeth. 'Be careful what you wish for, Sanasay Bayla. My lord has been expecting you.'

Bayla was led through streets of bone and dark granite where the dead were legion. The recently dead were engaged in the never-ending task of expanding Nagash's city, heaping bone and fashioned stone into new buildings. Skeletal warriors tramped the streets in rattling cohorts. Vampire lords rushed by in dark carriages. But though the city was huge, and populous, there was not a voice to be heard. The dead executed their duties in silence but for the hideous clattering of bones that echoed from every street.

They went to a black pyramid whose sides gleamed like

mirrors, and whose capstone was of pure wyrdstone. Deep inside, past numberless deathrattle regiments, Bayla was brought into a lofty hall. There sat Nagash, Lord of Death, surrounded by the ageless pomp of his court. Ghostly hand-maidens circled him, singing mournful songs.

'Who dares to tread the road of death to Shyish, and yet is not dead?' said Nagash.

Bayla's soul stepped forward boldly, the thread of his mortal life held lightly in one hand. 'It is I, great one, Sanasay Bayla of Andamar in Ghyran. I have come to seek an audience.'

Nagash's bony jaws clacked mirthlessly. 'To beg a favour, I think. What do you seek?'

'I have sought many years to find passage to Realms' End,' he said. 'I have come close to fulfilling my quest, but my way is barred.'

'Afrener, the wolf at the door,' said Nagash. 'He keeps guard.'

'I was told only death can kill him. You are death. Strike him down for me, so that I might look into the spaces beyond reality, and discover my true purpose in this life.'

Nagash stared at him with empty eye sockets. 'Sanasay Bayla, I know you as I know all mortals. All creatures pass through my domain sooner or later, and echoes of them are here forever. I never grant mortals favours, but for you I will make an exception, if only because you are a mage of awesome power. Agree to serve me for five hundred years and five days after your death, and I shall grant your desire, and slay this beast.'

'And what after five centuries?'

'You shall pass from Shyish, which for all its affinity with the beyond is but a Mortal Realm, into the Unknown Countries past my borders, as all souls ultimately must.'

Bayla knew better than to make foolish promises to a god, but he was desperate. 'Agreed!' he said.

'Then go, and do not forget our bargain,' said Nagash. He tilted his head to one side. Witchfire flickered in his eyes. 'It is done. But be swift, such a beast cannot remain dead for long. Awake!'

Sanasay Bayla returned to life with a moaning breath. He rolled onto his side, his restarted heart banging painfully behind his ribs, and vomited out all trace of the poison in his body. When he was done, he rose shakily, and looked upon the still corpse of Afrener. Mindful of Nagash's words, he hurried past. Shortly past the beast's reeking hindquarters, he came to the land of Realms' End.

What can be said of a place that defies mortal comprehension? Few have seen the Realms' End, and all who have have witnessed it differently. Bayla saw the far side of the mountains, sweeping down from unscaleable peaks to a short plain of bare rock. The horizon was close, the space beyond boiling with crimson and gold lights. There was no sky.

Full of relief that he would soon know his purpose, Bayla began a staggering run toward the edge of the worlds.

It was not far. He stopped where the land did, and peered down into a maelstrom of noise and fury. Amid roaring networks of lightning, lands were being born, coming into being fully formed, with forests, rivers and cities upon them, and no doubt peoples and histories too. They began as small floating islands, but grew quickly as more land solidified from the energy around them. Enlarged, the worldlets sank under their own weight, spinning slowly back toward the edge of Ghyran. At some preordained depth, they vanished in a burst of light, and so the process continued. Three lands were born while Bayla watched.

But of his purpose, he could see no sign. Searching up and

down the uncanny shore, he spied a robed figure clutching a staff in three hands. Bayla did not recognise its sort, and was suspicious of it, but having no option he made his way toward it.

'Sanasay Bayla,' the creature said raspingly as the mage halted a staff's length away. 'You have come to discover your purpose in life.' Its robes were a crystal blue, and a stylised eye topped its staff.

'I have,' said the mage.

'Here the worlds of Ghyran are born from nothing. This is a place is of purest magic. Everything can be seen. Behold!' said the creature. It opened out its arms, and pointed to the roiling energies beyond the final shore.

A vision of Bayla as a wise lord appeared, surrounded by adoring subjects.

'To be a king?' he asked the being. 'Is that my purpose?'

'More. Watch!' commanded the creature.

A procession of images paraded through the sky. Bayla saw himself in his library, moving faster than the eye could follow as time accelerated and the years coursed through the land of Andamar. New buildings sprouted, fashions changed. Wondrous devices were installed around the city, but Bayla did not age. His library grew in size and content. Knowledge unbounded filled his mind, he felt an echo of what he might learn, and was amazed. The great and the wise of many nations and peoples consulted with him. His name was known across time and in every realm. He watched avidly, eyes wide, and yet, and yet... There was something missing.

'Where is my wife?' he asked. 'My family?'

'They are not what you desire,' said the creature. 'Else why would you be here?'

The thing's words rang falsely, and Bayla set his powerful

mind to work on the stuff of creation where the vision played. He found it easy to manipulate. The creature shrieked out a spell, but its staff flew from its hand at a thought from Bayla and he refocused the scrying. The mage saw his wife and children grow old, unloved and neglected. As he succeeded, they failed, and were shunned. Palaces were constructed in his honour, while their graves were choked by vines and crumbled into the dirt. Realisation hit him. He wrenched the focus of the vision to the present, back to his home.

His wife waited for him. They had a new house, it seemed, and she bore all the trappings of success. Yet she looked sadly out over the minarets of Andamar. He was shocked at the signs of age that had settled on her, though she remained beautiful. His eldest son came to her side, to discuss some matter of business, and he saw he had been forced to become a man without his father to guide or nurture him.

Bayla stepped back in shock. 'I have been away too long!' he said. 'What am I doing?'

The creature was hunched over, two of its long-fingered blue hands clutching at the scorched third. 'Eternal life, ultimate power. These things are within your grasp,' it croaked. 'That is what you desire! Pledge yourself to my master, and they will be yours.'

The vision wavered, back to the hollow glories of an endless future. Bayla's face softened a moment at the opportunity offered, but hardened again.

'No. That is what I think I should want, but it is not.' He concentrated, and the image shifted back to the domestic scene. 'That is what I wanted, all along. To be a father and a husband. That is the purpose of a man in life. Power is fleeting. Family is eternal.' And it was. He saw son after daughter after son being born to the line of his people. Among them were

119

many who were mighty and wise, and Andamar prospered under their guidance. It seemed it would remain forever so, until suddenly fire rent the sky, and the city fell into ruin as a great cataclysm passed over all the realms.

'Too much!' screeched the creature. The vision fled like ripples over water. Bayla looked at the thing sharply.

'What was that?' he said, rounding on it. Arcane power glowed around his hands. 'I do not know what you are, but I know of your kind. You are told of in the oldest books, the things of the formless realms. The daemons of Chaos.'

The creature laughed, and raised its hands in conjuration. But Bayla was a mage beyond even the servants of Tzeentch, and he blasted it from existence. Its soul fled shrieking into the maelstrom, and passed beyond the fertile voids of Ghyran's edge, whence it would not return for thousands of years.

Bayla was troubled. War would come, one day.

Perhaps he had found two purposes.

He would warn the gods.

Turning away from the formless spaces, Bayla began the long journey home.

The mirror cleared of mist. Sigmar and Alarielle stared at their own faces caught in the silver.

'That was why he made us the mirror,' said Sigmar. 'Little attention we paid to his warnings.' The God-King shook his head in regret. 'Bayla was rare among men. He learned wisdom. With his gifts he could have risen and joined the ranks of the gods, but at the last he turned back. He understood that immortality is not to be craved, that the end of life gives the little span it has great meaning.'

'The gift of all mortals,' Alarielle said. 'They are free of the burden of life eternal. There is no surprise in this, and no new wisdom.'

'Every time they learn it, it is new,' Sigmar insisted. 'So few of them realise it from the beginning. Their lives are so short, their fear of death prevents them from recognising the gift they have.'

'You are immortal,' said Alarielle. 'They will find your sympathy false.'

'I did not seek to be so,' said Sigmar. 'I would have happily lived and died a mortal king. Some higher power had other plans for me.' He looked at her earnestly. 'Many chose Chaos because they had no other choice. They can be redeemed, even those whose hearts may seem black. But there are always those that seek to cheat death, and the lords of Chaos offer a way to do so, and are cunning enough to allow a few to ascend to become their immortal slaves. That is how they gained access to the realms in the first place. We became too distant from our charges, and they grew afraid. Chaos offered them immortality, of a sort. They did not know it was a trap.'

'Then what do you want of me?' said Alarielle.

'You have held yourself aloof for many ages, my lady,' he said. 'It would aid us all in defeating the four powers for good if you went again among the mortals. Teach them your wisdom. You of all the gods understand the ebb and flow of mortality best, and that death is but a turning of the way.'

'I do not know what becomes of the souls of men,' she said. 'Does even Nagash? You ask me to lie to them.'

'Not at all,' he said. 'I wish you to invest in them a love of all that is natural and alive, to appreciate its power and fecundity. If they learn to follow the rhythm of life's wondrous patterns, fewer of them will be tempted to fear its end. There always will be those who are incapable of fellow feeling, or whose greed outmatches their empathy,' he said. 'Many others can be saved by you.'

'I cannot do this,' she said. 'What is the point? Chaos rules already.'

'Cannot, or will not?' said Sigmar. 'You were worshipped all throughout Ghyran and beyond once, my lady. You can be again. You have become warlike to respond to a time of war, but you must reach inside yourself, and find that gentler creature you once were. We need to look beyond the end of this war, and prepare for peace. If we do not, then there will be another golden age, but soon enough Chaos will return and shatter the realms anew.'

'Victory and defeat has a cycle of its own,' she said. 'It is the way of things.'

'Maybe war and Chaos are the only constants of reality,' he said. 'But I do not have to accept it, and I will fight it for all time if I must. I cannot believe this is how the realms were meant to be. Send forth your spirits to speak with the wisest women and canniest men. Chaos has long used such missionaries against us. We shall do the same, and we have the advantage, for Chaos lies.'

Alarielle sighed, and the sound was of the wind in the boughs of a sleeping forest. She stared off across the plains of Azyr, still cloaked in the dark. The sun rose high enough to strike through the columns, casting long shadows across the city of the Highheim. When it struck Alarielle, she closed her eyes and basked in the warmth of it. Her body became translucent, and began to fade.

'I will do what I can, Sigmar Heldenhammer,' she said, her form becoming indistinct. 'But if I have learned one thing in my long existence, it is that humans rarely listen, and their males more rarely still.'

PANTHEON

The motes of light diffused. Her outline hung in the air a second. They flared and vanished, leaving a cloud of petals to drift to the floor.

Sigmar watched the day enter the city of the gods. As the golden light of Azyr's sun flooded the empty streets, he remembered a better time. He did not know if there were higher gods set over him to guide him as he shepherded his mortal kin, but he gave a silent prayer to them that finer times would return.

Then he too vanished, leaving the Highheim to the silence and the light.

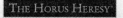

The Last Son of Prospero

Chris Wraight

'It has taken me a long time to find you,' said Kalliston.

Brother-sergeant Revuel Arvida looked up. The sun was hot, baking the mesa, making the sky shake. Rock formations in pale pink and sienna-brown marched out towards an empty horizon, flecked with broken bars of scrub.

'I do not understand why,' said Arvida, getting to his feet. 'I told you where I would be.'

'The desert is a big place.'

Both legionaries were coated in a fine layer of dust. Menes Kalliston, the taller, wore full battleplate save for the crested helm that hung at his belt on a bronze linked chain. Arvida wore fatigues, loose-fitting, white against the glare. His skin glistened with sweat. Away on the horizon, a line of gold-cranes flapped lazily into the noon haze.

'What did you learn?' asked Kalliston.

Arvida looked away from him, upwards, out into sunlight-blurred air. Something gauzy hung there, intermittently visible, caught like a reflection on the edge of vision. Look at it directly and it was gone – only in the half-glance could you see it, and then just for a moment.

'The sight is failing,' Arvida said. 'Falling out of the world. I see stone and sky, nothing beyond.'

Kalliston smiled. 'It will return. The Great Ocean has its tides.'

'Or it may dry up.'

'Does your tutelary give you no guidance?'

'When I am blinded, Ianius is blinded. When I see, he sees.'

Kalliston nodded. He reached up to wipe sweat from his brow. 'I wish I could give you more time, but orders have come – we are to make for the void.'

'Now?'

'So it seems.'

'Whose orders?'

'The primarch's.'

Arvida resisted a little longer. He had worked hard to control it, the need to probe, the tendency that had prevented his ascension through the Legion hierarchy, despite the power that even Ahriman had told him he possessed. The Thousand Sons were a deferential Legion. A respectful Legion. A Legion within which loyalty counted for more than in most.

'I do not understand it,' he said, despite himself. 'The Ocean is in turbulence – the few visions we still have are all of murder. The guard on Prospero must be maintained, now more than ever. Even you, brother-captain, have counselled the same.'

'So I have.'

'And so why–'

'What would you have me do?' Kalliston's severe face creased into another smile, but there was something under it – a weariness, perhaps, or possibly self-reproach. 'We make for the void. The skimmer is already on its way.'

Arvida looked away. The faint gauze flexed in the air above him, sparkling like sunlight reflected from water. Far out over the hard-beaten earth, the wind whipped dust into tiny vortices, *suspended for a heartbeat or two before scattering into nothingness. The deserts of Prospero were changing, turning green as irrigation schemes spread out from the nexus at Tizca. One day the barren lands would be as lush as gardens.*

'Why now?' Arvida asked.

'He will have his reasons.'

'Then he could share them.'

'Will he live?'

Arvida looked up. 'What?'

'Can he overcome the change?'

'I do not understand you.'

And then Kalliston was gone. Prospero was gone.

Only Ianius remained, hovering like a memory over the deeps, still sparkling in the doused sunlight.

'Why did we trust?' Arvida murmured, not expecting an answer, because he had asked that many times before, and had never yet had a good one.

'Will he live?' asked Khalid Hassan.

The chamber was pooled with darkness, so far underground that no sunlight had ever scraped across the wet stone. It should have been cold, but the flags underfoot were blood-warm and had been ever since the first wards had been broken. There were noises below, terrible noises, things that had not been heard since the oldest nights of the species' unguarded ignorance. Never ceasing, they clawed at the frail edge of sanity itself.

'Can he overcome the change?' Hassan pressed.

He felt the weight of responsibility. He had been the one to retrieve the subject from the V Legion warship *Lance of Heaven*. He had placed him in the stasis pod and arranged the warding patrols that had kept the Wolves of Fenris from detecting the transport. He had promised the weather-shamans of the White Scars that this warrior would be looked after, that he would remain intact long enough for rites of healing to be undertaken.

The vow had been honoured insofar as the Thousand Sons legionary had been taken into the care of the Sigillite, but whether it was fair to describe him as 'intact' remained moot.

The old armour had gone, peeled away during a surgery lasting six hours. The flesh within was bloated almost into obesity, mottled with burst blood vessels and discoloured into coralline outgrowths. What had once been thick muscle overlaid on a heavy bone-structure was now flabby, gilled, pulsing, slick with fats and sweats.

Many hands worked in that chamber. Orderlies brought in blood-cyclers and hypodermics, their faces swaddled in masks and their movements reminiscent of reverent monks. Robed adepts tended hissing respirator columns, their cowled faces never leaving gas-lenses running with esoteric data. Columns of incense rose up from strategically placed bronze bowls, making the chamber stink sweetly in a melange of blood and drained pus. Other figures, dark-robed, thin as whips, prowled the edges, reciting protective words in a language that had been dead long before the false dawn of Unification.

'Will you not give me an answer?' Hassan ventured, pressing the issue. The guilt hemmed him in, made his presence superfluous.

For a while longer he received none. The only one who could have responded was bent low with labour, just as he had been since the body had been brought in. His heavy cloak was damp with sweat. He looked old, that man, older than any living soul had any right to be. His spine was curved, his breath rattled, and yet the aura of power still curled out from beneath the frayed exterior, as if someone had tried to conceal the heart of a star within a scatter of rags.

Eventually, the robed man stood, unravelling, stretching out, until he seemed to stand taller even than Hassan. He turned deep-sunk eyes from the mire of blood. Malcador, called the Sigillite, steadied himself on the edge of the medicae slab, and drew in a thin breath.

'His soul wanders on the edge,' he said.

'Of life?' asked Hassan.

'Of damnation.' Malcador reached for a goblet and took a long swig, the clear contents tracing a thin line down his chin. 'It never could be cured from the outside. Not truly. That was the curse of it.'

He limped clear of the slab, feeling his way towards the far wall. In his absence the masked menials continued to tend the body, mopping it down with unguents and drawing arcane symbols on the heaving palls of flesh. Huge piped machines towered over them all, whirring, whispering, building up power and feeding it to crackling aether-traps.

Hassan followed his master. In the years since becoming one of the Chosen he had witnessed many testing things. He had traced paths across the deep void, snatching objects of value from under the bow-wave of the oncoming traitor advance, and that had brought him into contact with some measure of the terror that Horus had unleashed upon humanity. Of all of it, though, seeing the Sigillite's gradual erosion under the crippling burden of command was perhaps the hardest to accept. The Regent of Terra was burning up, burning out, breaking himself on the anvil of the Imperium's slow collapse.

'We knew his Legion suffered,' Malcador said, his breathing still shallow, his face sallow. 'Even before we discovered Prospero, we knew they were susceptible. We tried to aid them.

We thought it was some error in the gene encoding. I myself thought that for many years, and we expended much labour to isolate it.' He took another draught. 'It was not the gene encoding. It was something deeper in them, something that went to their core. In the end, only *he* could do what was necessary. We all believed that Magnus had cured them. His Father believed it. Why should we have doubted it? The Legions always needed their gene-sires – they had been designed to go together, and Magnus was the subtlest of them all.'

Hassan listened. Insights into the earliest days of the Great Crusade were given out rarely, and there were still secrets now shared only between the Sigillite and the Master of Mankind.

'But Magnus fell,' Hassan said.

'He dared too much. He was too proud. But still, even now, he is the only one who ever prevailed over the flesh-change. He cured his sons, once.'

'With sorcery.'

Malcador shot him a withering glance. 'Of course with sorcery. He was birthed from sorcery. This whole place was *built* upon sorcery. Give it whatever name you will, but the time is past for pretence.' He drank again, and the shaking in his hands receded a little. 'I will not apologise. There was no other path to tread. Even now, even *now*, fate has not quite run beyond us. He is here, and he still draws breath. His soul is not yet lost.'

'But... can anything... within *that*...'

'He lives, Khalid. Even now. We still have time.'

The ship was empty. Its holds echoed; its corridors flickered with broken lumens. The Geometric *had come out of the warp too soon, too close, and now the shields were breaking, the engines were beating, and something, something, was trying to get in.*

Arvida ran down the longitudinal spinal corridor, feeling the deck flex under his boots. His breathing rasped in his helm, his hearts thudded a tight rhythm. He had been asleep, taking a single hour of true rest before duty called again. The warning klaxons had woken him, ripping him out of a dream where all the worlds of the Imperium were as ashes, wreathed in unbroken clouds, their continents turned to broken glass.

He felt sick. Something was wrong. Reality had flexed and strained. The corridor's edges blurred and stretched out even as he ran down them.

Ianius was at his side, a diaphanous presence, calming him just by being there. He had forgotten if there had ever been a time when the tutelary had not been beside him. For a long time they had ceased to think of themselves as wholly separate entities. Ahriman had counselled that the companions were benign consequences of a greater understanding of the aether. But had they always been there, ready for discovery? Or had they been created somehow? Where did one soul end and the other begin?

Ianius did not like that speculation. It shimmered, shaking amid the sway and dance of emergency lights. Arvida found himself apologising even as he ran, requesting that it remain close, though he knew well enough that a tutelary never responded to reason.

A cacophony rang out from all around him – a hammering, a drumbeat of fists against the hull. He reached the bridge, and burst into its cavernous emptiness. Every servitor station was deserted. The command thrones turned slowly on their central columns. Out of the forward viewers he caught sight of a single world, lost in the blackness of the void, steadily burning.

Arvida approached the great crystalflex portal. Everything felt wrong. Everything felt false.

'I never saw it burn,' he murmured. 'We were not in time.'

He whirled around, running his blurred gaze across the bridge. Screens fizzed with static noise. Augur-relays gave no information.

The hammering was growing stronger. Above him, the observation dome blister cracked. A heavy interior panel bulged inwards, impelled by some enormous impact.

Arvida drew his blade, and black flame ran along the edge. Ianius twittered in panic, rippling under the flashing combat-lumens. More impacts banged in – throom, throom, throom – and the jabber of nameless voices began to filter through the damaged hull.

'He is my ward!' *came a roar, suffused with the stuff of the warp.* **'I have him under my countenance!'**

Arvida looked up, around, his blade drawn but with no enemy to slay. 'Where is Kalliston?' he asked, and instantly knew there would be no answer to that, for Brother-Captain Kalliston had never existed here either. The burning world on the scopes darkened, and the flames turned the dark red of old blood.

The hammering reached a crescendo. The ship was breaking.

Arvida felt himself dropping as the deck plates twisted, and he let the sword slip from his hands. Ianius ripped away, its silken haze blown apart by the rush of exploding atmosphere.

He tried to grip on to something, anything, but the universe was pulling itself apart.

The world burned, boiling the blood away into darkness.

'We were too late,' Arvida said, falling. 'We never saw it burn.'

Malcador had moved away from the door even as it cracked. Hassan drew his laspistol and backed up. There were shouts from the other side, panicked shots, the heavy clang of impacts on the portal's blast-shields.

'Behind me,' Hassan implored, moving to shield the Sigillite.

But Malcador did not move any further. 'Do not be foolish. There is not much that either of us could do to dissuade this one.'

The door cracked down its centre, smashed apart, its panels rammed back on their hinges. A warrior burst inside – a giant of a man, clad in ornate ivory armour, his eyes flashing with anger and untied black hair flying around his face.

'He is my ward!' roared the intruder, pointing accusingly at the Sigillite. 'I have him under my countenance!'

Malcador bowed. 'My lord Jaghatai,' he said. 'Try to calm yourself.'

The primarch swept towards him, as tall and gaunt as a hunting bird. His severe face was drawn with fury. 'I gave you leave to find a cure,' the Khan said. 'I did not give you leave to bring him *here*.'

'There was no alternative.'

'Look at him!' roared the Khan, swinging his heavy fist towards the quivering flesh-heap on the slab. 'See what he has become.'

Malcador remained patient. The expression on his ancient face, drawn tight over the bones, was as cruel as it was perceptive, and did not waver. He reached for his staff, leaning on it like an old man would, shuffling across to the slab and regarding the body on top of it with something close to pity.

'I cannot save him,' said Malcador. 'No one can, not now. He can still serve, though, in a manner of speaking. There is more at stake here than the life of a single warrior.'

The Khan shadowed Malcador, looking ready to tear the old man apart. 'I have a blood-debt to him. My Legion has a blood-debt to him. We would never have left the void were it not for his sacrifice. And I *will not* see him lost.'

Malcador paused, inclining his head a little. The noises – scrabbling and rending – continued under the floor, locked beneath the fragile barrier of the earth and stone below them. 'You told me of Dark Glass,' the Sigillite said. 'You know of the Thrones, and you guess the location of the greatest of them. There are walls in the Palace that have been breached and must be sealed. Your brother Magnus bears the shame of destroying wards that would have kept us secure, which is an irony, for it was he who was destined to guard those gates.'

'Magnus is dead.'

'No, Jaghatai, he is not. You know he is not. You met him yourself, on Prospero.'

'I met a shade.'

'One of many. The Crimson King has been broken, shattered like a mirror thrown in anger. It began when he breached the wards on Terra, and it was ended by the Wolf's wrath. No, Jaghatai, he is not dead. He has become *legion*.'

At that, the Khan drew back from Malcador, warily. 'What have you done here?'

'What needed to be done. Just as ever.' Malcador placed himself between the Khan and Arvida, defiant, both his clawed hands on his staff. 'The son of Magnus is here, brought to Terra by your hand. His sire was already here. Do not try to prevent this – the rites have already been completed, the protections set. It may fail, but it must be ventured.'

'This is an abomination.'

'I care not for the means,' said the Sigillite grimly. 'The gate must be guarded.'

Arvida stared into darkness. At first there was nothing to grip on to, just a blank void, hot and close. He could hear noises coming from far away, horrible noises, like screams pulled out too long until all the humanity had been wrung from them.

He felt his way forwards, and his hands pressed into crumbling earth. Up ahead was a glow, like muffled torchlight cupped within a sheltering palm. He was crawling, locked deep underground, progressing on his knees under some forgotten crypt. The air smelt foul and strange, and it was unfamiliar. He had never been on this world before, and had no idea how he had arrived there.

The closer he got, the more the glow of the light grew, until he could make out a narrow chamber hewn from the living rock. In it squatted something grotesque and enormous, man-shaped and yet far more than man-sized, hunched over a flickering red candle-flame. A mane of matted hair hung down its back, and caked soil blackened its exposed flesh.

Ianius was not there. His absence was an ache, but the presence of the giant made it seem somehow inconsequential. When Arvida saw the face – the lone eye, the thought-ploughed brow – a spark of fierce joy made him want to cry out.

'My lord!' he said, on his knees in the dirt.

The giant looked at him absently. The candle-flame burned in his palm, hovering in the air, a finger of fire in the deepest dark.

'Who are you?' he asked.

'Revuel Arvida, Fourth Fellowship of the Legion, my lord. Your Legion.'

'My Legion are all dead.'

'No, lord! No, they are not. I have seen them. And I saw you with them. I am sure of it.' Arvida paused, confusion slowing his thoughts. 'But then… How are you here? Where is this place?'

The earth shook briefly, disturbed by a tremor in the veins of rock below. Something like laughter rippled around the chamber.

'I do not remember you,' the giant said. 'Nor do I remember my name.'

'You are Magnus, the Crimson King. My liege, I have suffered much to see you again.'

The giant took that in slowly. In the flickering light of the single flame, he seemed translucent, like a shadow in winter. His great shoulders were hunched, his armour tarnished. The sigils upon his golden battleplate were all burned out, as if someone had taken a torch to them.

'That was one of my names,' the giant admitted at length. 'It no longer fits me.'

'The others are alive,' Arvida insisted. 'They can be found. Where are we? I have travelled through the empyrean, and I have seen the new Prospero forged in the abyss. There must be a path to it.'

The giant made no movement. Torpor dragged on his limbs. He looked into the heart of the flame moodily.

'Not for me,' he said. 'I ordered them all away. I left the gates open.'

Arvida remembered that. He remembered Kalliston telling him the command to leave had been given, but it was so long ago, lost in a world that had been destroyed and remade.

'Why, lord?' he asked, curiosity burning within him despite everything. He edged closer to his gene-sire, still on his knees. 'Why did you do it? If we had all been there, the whole Legion, then even the Wolves–'

'It was just.' The giant looked tormented, confused, as if recalling things from a dream that had already faded from memory. 'What they did to us, it was just. They were the punishment.'

'For what crime?'

'Oh, there were crimes.' The giant leaned forward, closer, keeping the flame cupped tight. 'I tried to cure you. I reached out, and I was answered. And then I had to warn my Father...' His lone eye suddenly lit up, and the flame flickered into greater life. 'But that broke me. I am not what you think.'

'You are the Crimson King.'

'No. He is gone. All that remain are... aspects.'

Arvida remembered something then – a warrior in gold and ivory, long ago, who had told him something similar, but it was so hard to remember, for the noises kept making the earth shake and he could hardly see and his head was full of the laughter of the things that were trying to burrow through the rock and get to him...

'We are on Terra,' said the giant, lifting his chin. 'That is

136

where I came, to warn my Father. The rest of me went back, but I remained.'

'Then I can help you,' said Arvida, urgently. 'I can help to restore you. I can show you the way they went.'

The giant smiled sadly. 'But you are not really here. Do you not see it, Corvidae? This is your death-dream.'

Arvida hesitated. He looked down at his hands. They looked solid enough. He could feel his hearts beating under his ribs, and could taste the loamy air of what must have been Terra's bedrock, the catacombs beneath the Imperial Palace.

'Where is your tutelary?' the giant asked him, now wryly amused.

'We are never apart,' said Arvida, cautiously.

'You are often apart. Until now you were apart for so long that you almost forgot his name.' The giant smiled again, but this time it was crooked. 'Such a conceit, those intelligences that whispered to us for so long. He's close behind you now, and I can hear him getting closer. He's pawing at the threshold. Do you see the danger?'

Arvida shrank back. 'He was my guide.'

'Or you were his. Come, you know how the Ocean is. Who leads whom? When all this is done, will it be that he was your tutelary, or were you his?'

Arvida began to feel cold. The clawing from under the earth was growing more intense. The soil began to tremble beneath his fingers, shifting like water.

'I am not dead yet,' he murmured.

'The moment comes,' said the giant.

The rock began to crack. Dust fell on both of them, and the roots of the world trembled. Arvida reached out, trying to grasp on to something solid. Ianius was gone. The flame guttered out, plunging him into utter blackness.

'I found you!' he cried, knowing how much it had cost, suddenly desperate not to lose it.

'You did,' said the voice in the dark, now growing in authority despite the collapse of all around them. *'So worry not – where you are going now, I can follow.'*

The Khan drew his tulwar, and the green light of the machines glittered on the curved edge of the blade.

'Get away from him,' he ordered.

But Malcador looked up, out at the arcane columns that towered over the slab, at the coils and the sigil-daubed ritual plates. The runes were glowing now, racing out of control. Aether-traps blew, showering the floor of the chamber with smashed crystal.

'Too late,' the Sigillite said, an edge of awe in his cracked voice, and he started to back away. 'He *comes.*'

The Khan pushed the Sigillite aside and reached out for the medicae slab.

He never made it. The aegis broke with a scream of torn atmosphere, hurling menials to the floor and cracking the stone flags. The chamber's interior erupted into eye-burning light, and the machines blew apart in unison. Hassan was thrown hard into the far wall, and Malcador was bent double. The Khan barely kept his feet, leaning steeply against the hurricane of raw energy.

Arvida's body was swamped in a nova of numinous light-spores, his outline lost behind a howl and a shriek of warp-rage. A chorus of screaming tore out – the roars of a tortured legionary, the bellows of a far deeper pain, and something else again, all overlapped, jumbled into a fractured mess of agony.

Malcador gained his feet, bracing his staff against the maelstrom and squinting into the inferno. 'The shard is here,' he breathed.

The dazzle of aether-brilliance blew itself out, revealing the husks of destroyed medicae stations at its epicentre – a broken slab, and a lone creature, man-shaped, staggering amidst the wreckage. It burned like the sun, a white hole in the world's fabric, writhing and shimmering, its shifting outline thundering like the planet's winds unleashed. It was screaming still, its back arched in the pain of its reanimation, its limbs jerking, its eyes streaming with strands of curling plasma.

The Khan strode towards it, fighting as if against a gale. 'Sorcerer!' he cried, holding out his empty hand. 'Come back to us!'

Malcador placed his staff-heel on to the chamber's floor, setting it against the tearing winds. 'No,' he muttered, signalling discreetly to the cowled figures recovering their positions all across the chamber. 'He must not fight it.'

At the sound of those words, the creature that had been Arvida suddenly turned. Its blazing eyes locked onto the Sigillite. It seemed to swell, to grow, sucking energy towards itself until it was nigh as huge as the Khan himself. It roared in pain and fury, threw its lightning-crowned fists out wide and sent a wall of kinetic force crashing into Malcador, hurling him across the buckling chamber floor.

The Sigillite struggled to get back to his knees, his face streaked with blood, his robes billowing. The unholy creation poured its soul out in a maelstrom of misery and anguish, stripping the runes from the metalwork, blistering the bronzed casings of the cracked warp-machines. The fires raged, and its empty eyes sprayed raw starlight, bleaching the stone as white as phosphor.

Malcador gasped against the cold power of it, but his disappointment was tinged with fear. 'Enough. His body cannot contain it.'

At some unseen psychic command, the ruined devices roared back to life. The coils crackled with plasma, the aether-traps started rattling again. Great runes embedded on the chamber walls flared into life, and the surviving menials screamed out a broken chorus of banishment and protection. A shudder rippled through the air, and tendrils of black-edged force crackled out from iron vanes embedded in the chamber's roof.

Stasis enveloped the abomination, crushing it back on its heels, stripping the air from its lungs and boiling it away. Malcador rose to his full height, and his staff now swam with overlapping layers of distortion. More hammered-iron runes surged into visibility, flaming in their stone-carved channels, their occult resonance drowning the furnace at the chamber's heart.

The onslaught abated. The waves of shriving force lessened; the figure at their heart reeled. A rapid flurry of changes swept across its diaphanous outer shell, cavalcades of faces, one after the other. Its limbs flexed and swelled and retreated, boiling like magma. Its mouth opened in a rictus of despair, and gouts of boiling flesh-matter slipped from its churning shoulders.

'It was worth the attempt,' the Sigillite said darkly, moving towards it, preparing the death-strike that would condemn them both. 'But it ends now.'

The sky was alive with souls. The dark rocks reflected them in glassy facets; the air shook from their elemental anger. Lightning as thick as tree boles, neon-silver, crashed among the soulstorm, fusing them, melding them, churning the sea of sentience into the raw stuff of Chaos. The stars wheeled overhead, faster than imagination, but they were no stars ever glimpsed by mortals.

Arvida held his blade, backing away, his heel slipping on the blood-slick rock. The spectre came after him, vast and shimmering, a glowing, fractured thing of pure psychic projection.

'Why resist?' *it asked, its single eye burning with cold fire. It carried a flame-wreathed sword that cleaved the air around it.* 'You know who I am, now.'

Arvida retreated further. On the far horizon was a dark tower, its sheer flanks riven by storms, its summit lost in the torment of the warp.

'I know only what you told me,' *said Arvida, warily, trying to clear his head, trying to make sense of the torment, the whirl of energy pulsing through his veins. He felt as if he might split apart, dissipated into flying atoms, and yet his armour was still intact; his blade still hummed with a nimbus of luminous force.* 'And you are not what you were.'

The spectre came after him, towering into the storm-racked skies, its rippling crown snagging at the pull of burning souls.

'I am potential. Just as you are, my son.'

'I am no one's son,' *said Arvida, and the words sent shards of ice into his heart.* 'I spurned those who would have taken me, and I never sought those I lost. Not hard enough, at least.' *His head was thick, his veins hot. It felt like he was on fire, being consumed from within, gnawed away by ancient magicks, and yet he could still stand, he could still hold a blade, he could still defy.*

'You have been in pain for too long,' *the spectre said, sweeping higher, closer.* 'Let i-t end.'

He remembered more. He remembered the long, long nights in shattered Tizca. He remembered the coming of the sons of Chogoris, and the dragon-helmed one who severed the dark. He remembered the long war of loss, the tarot deck that he took from its master and gave to his friend.

And he remembered the path into hell that had taken that friend's life, snuffing out a great and noble soul on the altar of survival. Through it all, the pain, the pain, *constant and unwavering, never letting him rest, never letting him grow. His only mantra had been to keep going, to keep fighting, never to trust, never to find sanctuary.*

There had been his friend's words. I hope you can stop running now, brother.

Arvida felt the rocks shift under his weight. He half-turned to see a crevasse opening up at his back, wide and yawning, falling away into darkness. The storm crashed overhead. The souls screamed. The stars wheeled faster.

He held his ground on the edge, watching doom catch up with him.

'You have nowhere else to go. I told you – this is your death-dream.' *The spectre's profile sheared, sliding, flickering.*

'I did not fight on Prospero,' Arvida said, feeling the shame of it all over again. 'I had to live long enough to reach Terra.'

'You *are* on Terra.'

'And it is not enough.'

The spectre's sword was lifted now, its long curved blade like the one borne by the dragon-warrior, and for a moment Arvida thought he heard the Khan's voice amid the storm, crying out in rage just as he had done when Yesugei had sacrificed himself.

'You have tried to preserve it,' *the spectre said.* **'You kept your armour, but the others who survived will leave that behind. You were the last son of Prospero, but it means nothing now. Prospero is no more, and all must change.'**

'Except you,' said Arvida. 'They wish to preserve you.'

'It cannot be done.'

'Then all is for naught.'

'Nothing I did was for naught.' *The spectre's blade disintegrated then, sliding out of existence like a sigh, and the ghost extended its empty hand.* **'Where is your tutelary, my son?'**

Arvida whirled around, suddenly feeling the lack again, but the black skies only screamed back at him. 'I never asked him what he was,' he said, bewildered. 'We asked them so many questions, but never that.'

He was tired now. The exhaustion of years seeped into him. The spectre came closer, reaching out for him, and the strange stars turned wildly above it.

'You know the answer, though.'

The spectre slid over him, draining his agony, excising it all in a slough of blessed annihilation.

'You are Corvidae. You have always known the answer.'

Even then, he could have resisted.

'What remains, then?' he asked, his consciousness finally slipping away, caught between the grief and the anguish of it. 'After this, what remains?'

'Rebirth,' *said the broken shard of Magnus the Red.*

The Khan leapt forwards, throwing himself at the rows of warp-machines and crystal columns, smashing them, ripping out cables and demolishing the aether-traps.

Malcador lurched after him. 'It failed!' he cried, trying to restrain him even as the choristers scattered before the rampaging primarch. 'It cannot be allowed–'

'He was my *ward!*' roared the Khan, shaking the Sigillite off and toppling a rune-scored column. He spun around, powered blade in hand, obliterating the rows of bubbling philtre vials. 'He was under my countenance!' The glowing sigils blew out into smoking lumps of metal, the lightning-vanes cracked. 'And he will have his chance!'

The Sigillite moved to intervene, his staff making the air ripple, only to face the Khan's crackling tulwar.

'One more step,' the primarch warned, his voice as cold as the void, 'and your head will crown a spike on the roads to Khum Karta.'

Startled, Malcador pulled back, then snapped his gaze over to the reeling abomination.

'Jaghatai, what have you done?' he asked, his voice low.

The Khan turned to look at it. Hassan, dragging himself to his feet, gazed at it. Held in check by the primarch's promise of violence, the remaining menials cowered in fear, silent and staring.

Freed of the suppression fields and null-wards, the agonised amalgam was moving again. The thing's features morphed, running into one another in a fluidity of pain. Tremendous energy pulsed within it, spilling out of its mouth, its eyes, its outstretched fingers, but there was no control. It was a riot of purples, blues and other colours that had no name.

'You know me, brother, sorcerer,' the Khan said, coming closer yet, weathering the fires that spat and splintered. 'You crossed the realm of the gods. You are *not* ended here.'

The creature shrank back, clutching at invisible nightmares, and the fires began to gutter. The kaleidoscope of faces slowed, until there were only two left – a bloated flesh-changed horror and a one-eyed ghost, melding into one another and back again with bewildering speed.

Malcador limped closer, a mix of foreboding and curiosity on his withered face, but made no further move to interfere.

The creature began to change again, blotching and erupting. Its skin blackened, burning with psionic fire, sucking inwards then blowing out in smaller eruptions of blood and bone. Its screaming became truly pitiable then, a mewl of existential terror. Its shell flexed obscenely, as if trying to accommodate something too great for mortal bounds. Flesh melded, sinews knitted, bone cracked and re-formed, all forged under the white-hot burn of the undiluted empyrean.

Slowly, though, the overspill of energy furled back, solidifying into hard knots of matter. The creature crouched low, lost in its own world of destruction and creation, sporadic flames still running down its spine.

Jerkily, haltingly, it stood again, pulling itself to its full height, casting off the slough of suffocating warpfire, and revealed itself, at the end, to be a man.

He was whole. He was living. He had a stocky, vigorous frame, bull-necked, with an angular jaw, taut flesh over heavy bones. The sores were gone, the lesions healed. He was naked, all his tattered robes burned away, and his body was the slab-muscled hulk of a legionary. One eye was swollen, little more than a slit amid puffed scar tissue, while the other was hale. Power crackled across his new-made skin, a play of potency that hurt to look upon. The air trembled around him, shimmering like the heat-distortion of Prospero's old deserts.

When he looked up, the agony had gone.

Malcador said nothing. The last debris from the aether-traps clattered to the stone. The blood-cyclers ticked to a halt. The devotional flames wavered in their bowls.

The Khan looked hard at the figure before him. The face was at once Arvida's and not Arvida's, at once Magnus' and not Magnus'. There was no primarch there, but also no mortal man. They faced one another for the space of many heartbeats, neither moving, neither speaking.

Curls of energy circled around the new creation, dancing like corposant. Slowly, it flexed its hands, one then the other, looking at itself in a kind of mute wonder. Every physical gesture was halting, accompanied by the extrasensory tang of the warp.

Malcador kept his staff held two-handed, ready to use. The build-up of power in the chamber made the air fizz, primed to ignite.

Slowly, the Khan lowered his blade. His eyes narrowed, as if he were scrutinising a falcon for the hunt. This was no shadow-primarch in a host shell, nor was it a flesh-changed aberration. It was something else. Something new.

'You are not Arvida,' the Khan said at last.

The figure looked at him. 'Not entirely.'

'The sickness?'

'Gone.'

Malcador remained defensive. 'Do not approach him,' he warned.

'I am not what you intended, Sigillite,' the flawed creation said. 'I know what that means for you, and I am sorry. Believe me.'

Malcador looked briefly surprised, then gave a wry, defeated smile. 'The subtlest of them all,' he murmured.

The Khan sheathed his blade, unsure whether he faced a comrade, a brother, or both. 'What shall I call you?'

The creation looked up at the primarch and there was recognition there, a recognition that recalled the glory of the Great Crusade, a recognition that sprung from the ashes of lost Tizca. Some memories had evidently survived the process, while others were little more than half-remembered dreams.

For the first time in a long time, though, there was clearly no pain, and that changed things. When he spoke, his voice was soft, assured, bipartite.

'Know me by the name I always had,' he said. 'Call me Ianius.'

Into Exile

Aaron Dembski-Bowden

10

Gritty ochre dust clings to the dead warrior's open eyes. A shadow retreats from his stilled form, something immense yet hunched, something with rattling joints and grinding metal claws. It strides away, limping badly, its orders unfulfilled, its masters informed.

The legionary lies in the dirt, his duty done.

9

The scholar sits hunched in the chamber of stinking steel and bleeding bodies, breathing in the scorched scents of mangled automata and riven human flesh. The creature on his shoulder bears no small resemblance to a species of simian detailed in the archives of Ancient Terra. Its name is Sapien. The scholar named it himself when he constructed the creature from vat-cloned fur and consecrated metals.

The psyber-monkey gives a worried chitter at their surroundings. The scholar feels no such unease, only disgusted

147

irritation. He sneers at these charnel house surroundings, this place of the ruined and the wounded that is supposedly his salvation.

The arched walls shake around him. Outside the ascending ship, the sky of Sacred Mars is on fire. Far below, Nicanor will be dead by now. Butchered, no less. The fool.

Arkhan Land huddles like some filthy refugee amidst the other survivors, praying to the Omnissiah that the reek of their cowardice and failure won't infect him.

Sapien scampers to Land's other shoulder. He chitters again, the tone wordless yet curiously inquisitive.

'He *was* a fool,' the scholar murmurs, idly stroking the cog-like vertebrae plates that made up the little creature's spine. 'Space Marines,' he snorts the words. 'They are all fools.'

But even to himself, those words ring a little hollow this time.

8

Nicanor stares into his slayer's eyes. His own blood marks the bulbous golden domes of the war machine's visual actuators, blood that he coughed into the thing's face right after it drove the crackling, motorised spear through his breastplate. It keeps him aloft, impaled, his boots scarcely scraping the dust that makes up the useless yet priceless Martian soil. Each scuff smears away the red-brown regolith to reveal greyer earth beneath – a secret of the Red Planet concealed mere inches beneath the surface, yet unknown to most capable of conjuring the world's image in their imaginations.

The machine leans in closer, the domes of its insect eyes inspecting the prey, recording Nicanor's face and the markings upon his armour. The dying warrior hears the clicking whirr of an open transmission sluice as his killer exloads its findings to its distant masters.

This is prey. It knows that in the processes of its murderously simple consciousness.

But this is the wrong prey.

Nicanor swallows the pain. He doesn't cower from it and he refuses to let it consume him. Pain is felt only by the living, and thus it is nothing to regret. Pain is life. Pain can be overcome as long as breath resides in the human, and transhuman, body. He will die, he knows this, but he will not die ashamed. Honour is everything.

Blood falls from Nicanor's clenched teeth as the war machine shakes him, seeking to dislodge him from the toothed length of its spear-limb. The lance is buried too deeply in his innards, clutched by reinforced bone and armour plate, and refusing to easily come free. He feels his left boot connect with his fallen boltgun, the ceramite clanking against the gun's kill-marked metal body. Even if he could twist to reach for it without tearing himself in two, the weapon is empty. Through his reddened gaze he still sees the scorched pockmarks cratering the robot's head, where every bolt he fired found its target.

The war machine lowers its spear, slamming the impaled warrior hard against the dusty ground, and its taloned foot crunches down on Nicanor's limp form for leverage. With a brace and a wrench of machinery joints, the lance tears free in a fresh scattershot of bloody ceramite and cooling gore.

The disembowelling also pulls the last breath from what remains of Nicanor's body. He stares up, strengthless and silent, and he sees nothing in the robot's implacable eye domes. There is no hint of intelligence or sign of who might be watching through the automaton's retinal feed.

His greying gaze slides skyward, slipping from the hunched and bolt-blasted carapace of his mechanical slayer. There, rising into the embattled sky, is the silhouette of the scholar's transport vessel.

It would be poetic to say that this is Nicanor's final thought, and victory is his final sight. Neither is true. His final thought is of the ruination of his breastplate, where the symbol of the Raptor Imperialis had shown so proud in ivory upon the golden-yellow plate. His last sight is of Mondus Occulum, where subterranean foundries and bolt shell manufactories burn beneath the Martian rock, and where the last of his brothers' gunships stream into the sky.

The dust in the air begins to settle over his armour, upon his torn body, even on his eyes as they twitch one last time, yet fail to close.

The war machine casts a shadow across his corpse as it records his demise.

7

Land runs, breath sawing from his mouth, spit spraying with each heave. His boots clang up the gang-ramp, which rises already beneath his panicked tread. He doesn't look back, not to bid the Space Marine farewell, not to bear witness to the warrior's final moments. The hammer-crash of Nicanor's discharging boltgun is the last thing that Land hears before the hatch grinds inexorably closed.

There, in the fresh dark, he collapses to his hands and knees, all dignity abandoned. Shaking hands drag the multilens focusing goggles from his face.

Safe, he thinks. *Safe.*

And for some reason the thought feels almost treasonous.

Perhaps a lesser man might consider it guilt. The niggle of a weak soul's conscience, knowing that Nicanor is still out there, selling his life to buy Land's survival.

But pragmatism drowns any pathetic stirring of morality. Conscience and guilt are concepts brought into being by those too meek to face up to their failures, seeking to mark their hesitations as virtues.

He has to survive. That's the beginning and end of it. He matters infinitely more than a single legionary. Nicanor's own actions prove the truth of it.

'*Ascension,*' comes a servitor's bland tones over the chamber-wide vox. The transport begins its rise in shaking inelegance.

Arkhan Land weaves through a compressed sea of moaning, wounded forms, and sits with his back to the chamber wall. Sapien squawks an entirely unsimian sound as he takes his place upon his master's shoulder.

6

'*Run!*' Nicanor's voice, even weakened, is a roar above the wind. '*Run, damn you!*'

He turns with his boltgun braced against his shoulder, trusting that the technoarchaeologist's arrogance and fear will serve even if Nicanor's command fails. The war machine lopes and lurches closer, leaping over the wind-smoothed grey rocks that lie across the Martian surface like the tumbledown shamanic stone circles of Old Earth.

And it is the same machine. It bears the scars that Nicanor already inflicted upon its armour plating with bolter and bomb back in the Mesatan Complex. It sprints forwards on backward-jointed legs, its chain-toothed limbs revving in the silence of its empty rotor cannons.

Nicanor's boltgun barks in futility. Explosive shells strike true, detonating against the stalker-killer's insectoid cranial housing, doing little more than jerking the head with its bulbous golden eyes to the side.

He knows he can't kill it. He knows he doesn't need to. Sigismund didn't send him here to kill this thing.

He drops the bolter the instant his retinal display chimes that his magazine is empty. His power sword flares to life in both hands before the gun has even hit the ground.

The hunting machine could circle around him if its cognitive processes choose to do so, but threat sensors flicker with suggestions of caution. This prey has thwarted it once already, and time is short. The kill must be now, or it will be never.

It charges, janky legs clanking. Spear-limb joints bunch up, driving back into their piston housings. It leaps, emitting a scrapcode shriek for want of a true battle cry.

Nicanor hurls himself to the side, rolling in the dust and dirt, defacing his damaged armour further by occluding the proud symbols that have stood upon the ceramite for over three decades. His injuries leave him slow, slower than he has ever been. He comes to his knees in a sense-lost haze of disorientation, thrusting upwards with the blade.

It bites. It bites deep, with the snarling kiss of an aggravated power field knifing into sensitive mechanics. Sparks fly in place of blood's spray. He feels the machine buckle above him, its thwarted core straining, the sword buried in the underside of its hip joint threatening to plunge the beast-machine to the ground.

He must live, Nicanor thinks, tasting blood in his mouth. *And he will.*

He pulls the blade free from the crippled war machine in exalted silence, stoic to the last, leaving the bellowing of war shouts for the warriors of lesser Legions that require such pageantry. The sword snaps near the hilt as the machine whines and staggers back.

Nicanor is rising, turning, just in time for the stalker-killer's primary limb to emit a peal of crunching thunder as it pounds through the Space Marine's plastron. It shatters the reinforced casing of his fused ribs, kills the motive force of his Mark II battle armour as it lances through the suit's back-mounted power pack. It annihilates both of his hearts, two of his three lungs, the progenoid gland in his chest.

He coughs blood as the crippled machine drags him up before its alien face. He is grinning when he hears the engine cacophony from the transport lifting off.

'He lives,' he tells his killer. These will be his last words. 'You have failed.'

5

They are almost to the landing site when Arkhan Land realises the severity of the Space Marine's wounds. The warrior's limp becomes a stagger, his stride arrested as he seeks to pull his helmet clear and breathe without the filtration grille. It comes free to reveal a dark face with a typical Terran equatorial skin shade, blood riming the gritted teeth. It is the first time Land has seen the warrior's features. He makes no comment on this because he doesn't care.

Since emerging from the underground complex, there has been no sign of their pursuer. Ahead across the rusty desert, the orbital lander sits with its gang-ramps down, accepting evacuees and materiel in a shuffling and stumbling trickle.

It is not the ship that Land would have chosen for himself. Nor would he associate with the scavengers and dregs now boarding it, had he any other choice. But it is said that beggars cannot be choosers. The same can be said for refugees.

Without even realising he is doing it, Land shields Sapien from the gathering wind, holding the psyber-monkey in the folds of his magisterial, crimson robe. Sapien accepts this treatment, displaying a fanged maw no natural simian had ever possessed. The expression may possibly be a smile.

'Space Marine,' Land calls over the wind.

'All is well,' the towering warrior calls back. Plainly, it is a lie. All is anything but well. Nicanor touches a gauntleted hand to the shattered ceramite at his side. The armoured fingers come away red.

'Your kind do not bleed this much,' Land accuses him with lazy vehemence. 'I have read the physiological data myself. In detail.'

'We bleed this much,' the Imperial Fist replies, 'when we are dying.' He gestures to the segmented evacuation craft being slowly abraded by the rising wind. 'Keep moving, Techno-archaeologist Land.'

But Land doesn't keep moving. He fixes his multilens goggles over his eyes, looking back the way they came. Not for the first time, he wishes he was armed. His collection of antiquities boasts many archeotech weapons, the pinnacle of his hoard being a deliciously beautiful sidearm with humming aural dampeners, rotating magnetic vanes, and the capacity to fire micro-atomic rounds. But it – along with many of his possessions – is elsewhere. A significant portion of his priceless finds are safely secured and await him once he reaches the Ring of Iron that surrounds Mars in a sacred dockyard halo.

Even so, he is already cataloguing the innumerable precious items he has been forced to abandon on the planet today.

Evacuation is such a dirty word.

Sapien hisses in his cradle of robes. Land nods as if the sound held some kind of sense, adjusting his goggles' visual range with a clicking twist of a side dial.

'Space Marine,' he says, looking over the dusty plain behind them. 'Something is approaching from the southern ridge.'

It *had* followed them through the complex, after all. All of those byzantine twists and turns, hoping to put distance between themselves and their foe, had been nothing more than wasted meandering.

The wounded warrior clutches his weapons tighter as he turns. Land hears the click of Nicanor's eye lenses resetting, cancelling their zoomed view.

This ends now, Land thinks. *One way or another, this ends now.*

'Get to the ship,' the Space Marine says. And when Land moves at a slow, exhausted jog instead of a sprint, Nicanor's temper finally flares. *'Run!'* he says, his voice a crack of breaking arctic ice. *'Run, damn you!'*

4

They walk through tunnels of flickering light, the power systems feeding the Mesatan Complex failing one by one, falling to abandonment or treachery. Their passage is sung in the sound of their footsteps – the technoarchaeologist's ragged, tired tread, and the Fist's own fading gait.

Nicanor no longer disguises his limp. Fluid leaks from where the robot's withering storm of solid slug gunfire savaged his armour plating. It's worst in several medial and inferolateral locations that he doesn't need his retinal display to describe. He can feel the grind of abused metal against – and *inside* – injured flesh, without the aggressive chime of warnings across his visor display.

He can smell his own wounds, smell their coppery open-
ness from a refusal to heal with the expected speed. That isn't
a good sign.

'You said there was a ship,' Arkhan Land says without looking back at the warrior.

'A sub-orbital,' Nicanor confirms.

'Already it sounds like some grotesque last gasp for refugees.'

That is exactly what it is, Nicanor thinks. 'The arrangements
were made with whatever resources were available.'

'Arranged by whom?' The technoarchaeologist, a wheezing
shape of rippling crimson robes, radiates an aura of dis-
approval. 'By you?'

'First Captain Sigsimund,' Nicanor replies, 'and Fabricator
Locum Zagreus Kane.'

Still he doesn't turn, yet Nicanor hears the smirk in Land's
tone. 'Fabricator *General* Zagreus Kane now, I'll wager? Omnissiah preserve us from that punishingly dull creature and his
limited vision.'

Nicanor casts back a sweat-stinging gaze into the flickering
depths of the corridor behind. He sees nothing. No new warning chimes pulse on his retinal feed beyond the ones screaming
of his injuries. His auspex scanner remains silent.

Corridor by corridor, they rise through the complex. Nicanor feels his limbs growing leaden as his body assimilates the
adrenal sting of the medicae narcotics flooding his system. The
strength they granted over the last hours deserts him by incre-
ments, inviting back the weary burn of his wounds.

'I've never encountered one of those automata before,' Nicanor says.

Arkhan Land turns his sharp features back upon his armoured
companion. Amusement gleams in the scholar's half-lidded

eyes. 'A Space Marine with a passion for idle chatter? My, my, my. The surprises never cease.'

Nicanor bridles. 'I seek answers, not conversation.'

Land gives an unpleasant smile before turning to the tunnel ahead. The psyber-monkey on his shoulder noisily crunches on a steel ingot.

'It is a Vorax,' the technoarchaeologist says in an arch tone. 'This one has been modified by a forge-noble to suit his or her own purposes, I've no doubt, but the chassis is that of a Vorax automaton. They rarely see use in the hosts of the Great Crusade anymore. We release them into the forge cities when overpopulation becomes a concern. They are,' he adds with a refined air, '*occasionally* tasked for assassination protocols. But only against targets of sufficiently high priority.'

Nicanor reads the pride in the scholar's voice. The man's arrogance knows no bounds.

'Who would want you dead, Technoarchaeologist Land? The men and women you were keen to remain and face alone?'

The robed man scratches his hairless crown – for no reason Nicanor can discern the psyber-monkey mimics the gesture, scratching its own head. 'There you've asked a question of staggering ignorance, Space Marine. A great many of my contemporaries would enjoy the notion of me breathing my last. Not all, of course. But enough. On both sides of this new war.'

Nicanor grunts at the pain in his side. Land takes it as a question.

'And why, you ask?' the technoarchaeologist carries on, though Nicanor has asked no such thing. 'Because I am *Arkhan Land*. Jealousy motivates them. Jealousy forged in their own insecurities. I suspect that says it all.'

The Imperial Fist says nothing. He's seen unmodified humans do this before – the propensity that even overconfident souls have for fear-babble in times of duress.

When they emerge at last into the dubious light of the Martian dawn, the Zetek alkali plains stretch out before them.

Nicanor gestures to a rise in the landscape. 'The ship waits over that ridge.'

3

It's difficult not to be insulted, really. A single Space Marine.

The Mesatan Complex unlocks and unfolds before them via a series of grinding, whirring doors resembling void-sealed bulkheads – a design choice that Arkhan Land attributes to radiation shielding and disaster containment rather than a consideration of security. Given what's happening across Mars – the insanity so poorly draped in the rags of revolution – he's unsurprised that the complex has been automatically locked down.

'We are being followed,' the Space Marine says at one point.

Land, who has heard nothing at all, gives a tired grunt. The pace is punishing. He has no augmentations. His throat is raw. His legs are burning.

The technoarchaeologist and his companion move swiftly, their boots striking echoes through the empty colonnades. It's a disappointment, to be sure. Despite using the deserted complex as nothing more than a subterranean avenue for the sake of convenience, Land can't help but feel an irritated melancholy at what he's seeing. The emptiness reminds him of the underground mantle-cities he so keenly explores, where his only companions in the Search for Knowledge are the dungeon-slaved defence systems of a forgotten age, and the serenity of his own thoughts.

Will he ever know that peace again?

And how long will the power last here in Mesatan? Without the complex's thrall workers, the air filtration gargoyles mounted within each chamber will cease to breathe sooner rather than later. Anyone still down here within a few days will likely expire from asphyxiation.

And this, Land reflects, would be a truly pointless place to die.

On the run from his own contemporaries, no less. Omnissiah have mercy, it is almost maddening enough to be amusing.

The Imperial Fist leads the way across a bridge stretching over a storage repository, where thousands of crates and containers make up a township below.

A single Space Marine...

Land draws breath to ask why the Imperial Fist is alone, why it was deemed appropriate for a mere lone warrior to defend and escort him... when their pursuer makes itself known.

The Vorax strikes when they're halfway across the span with nowhere to go, its nasty and near-feral cognition aware that they can hardly leap from the high bridge to safety.

The first sign of its presence is when the walkway judders on its support beams, and both Land and the Fist break into a run. Land's frantic stride takes him forward in flight – not for a deluded second does he believe that the machine is here to save him – and the legionary immediately turns back the way they came.

The Imperial Fist is a blur of grinding armour as he passes Land, while the technoarchaeologist is a flapping silhouette of austere robes and simian howling, the latter from Sapien rather than Land himself. Even as he's fleeing for his life, Land feels a tickle of embarrassed dread for believing that they had lost their pursuer for good.

'Get behind me,' the Fist demands.

Land obeys without thinking. The Vorax leans into its awkwardly graceful sprint, its bulbous sensoria-domes locked in a cold, animal glare. Its rotor cannons cycle to life, spear-limbs retracting in something akin to bestial eagerness, ready to launch forth.

The Imperial Fist stands between Land and the automaton. The Space Marine fires first.

Land has never seen the Legiones Astartes fight before. Not outside of visual recordings, with his own eyes. Despite all the ways in which his work has aided – *revolutionised* may not be too strong a word, really – the armouries of the Legions, the warriors themselves and their various capabilities have never particularly interested him, beyond the extent of the Omnissiah's genius in creating them. He studied their physiology insofar as he was able, but a great deal of it was sealed away behind Imperial edict, and much of what he *could* access was bland propaganda.

He left it at that. Frankly, he didn't care.

War, to Arkhan Land, has always been a notion of excruciating boredom.

Land's passion is for how the rediscovered secrets of the past may brighten the future, rather than the tedious brutalities of the present. Space Marines are tools and they fulfil their role with uninspired aplomb.

This one is nevertheless an impressive specimen of the battling art. He opens up with a tremendous crash of bolter-fire, every shot impacting against the Vorax's armour plating, not a single shell going wide. All the while he backs away, keeping his bulk between the machine and its kill-target, twitching and buckling under the rattling slug-fire from its rotor cannons and yet refusing to fall.

Sparks fly from the Imperial Fist's armour. Scraps of ceramite clatter in steaming shards to the walkway gantry. He is being drilled. No other words sum up the destruction inflicted upon the towering warrior. He is being drilled by gunfire.

Bullets whine and buzz past where Land cowers in the warrior's shadow. They spank and clang off the walkway's railings, inches from where he stands.

Still the boltgun booms.

'Nicanor–' Land says. It is the first and last time he will speak the Imperial Fist's name.

Nicanor fires one-handed, grunting as his blood mists in the air. His free gauntlet reaches for the melta bomb bound to his back.

'Run,' the Space Marine orders, and pulls the device.

'That will not–'

'For the bridge.' Nicanor keeps his armoured pauldron facing the advancing, reloading foe, with his helmet half-masked behind it. 'Not for the machine. Run.'

He's going to blow the br–

Land runs.

2

'You are the technoarchaeologist Arkhan Land,' says Nicanor.

It isn't a question. The man he addresses is slight of build, sparse of hair, wears multilens wide-spectrum visualiser goggles lifted high up on his forehead, is clad in the layered robes of a senior adept over the more practical travelling bodysuit and rugged armour of a mendicant Martian, and is in the company of an artificimian – a psyber-monkey – that watches Nicanor with clicking picter-eyes.

Additionally, the man's facial features exactly resemble the image files that Nicanor has stored in his retinal display. This is unquestionably Arkhan Land.

Nicanor can see that the man is afraid, betrayed by an accelerated heart rate and the sheen of fear-sweat on his brow. But there is pride here; Arkhan Land may be a non-combatant and in fear for his life – and, indeed, his entire way of life – but he stands tall and defiant even with a tremble in his limbs.

This is good, Nicanor thinks in his dispassionately amused way. It is good to admire someone that you may have to die for.

'I am he,' the sharp-eyed human replies. 'And, dare I ask, which side you are on, Space Marine?'

Nicanor stiffens at the insult of the man's words, though given the circumstances they are understandable enough. 'I am Sergeant Nicanor Tullus of the Seventh Legion.'

Land sneers, rejecting the answer. 'That tells me nothing but your name and your lineage, Space Marine.'

'I am loyal to the Emperor.'

At that, the technoarchaeologist exhales something between a sigh of relief and a breath of irritation. 'I trust you are here to "save" me, then. Well, I commend you for your efforts in locating me, but those efforts have been in vain. I am not leaving my home world. Sacred Mars is aflame with heathenism, true enough, but it is my home.'

Nicanor expected this. He commits precious seconds looking around the laboratory, seeking any sign of weaponry capable of causing him harm. There appears to be precious little in the way of threat amongst the near-preternatural degrees of clutter. Arkhan Land is hailed as a genius, but if his mind is as disordered as the space he inhabits, then it is a chaotic genius indeed that resides behind those unhappy features.

'My brethren are assisting in the defence and evacuation of the Mondus Occulum forge. I was assigned–'

Land barks a laugh, speaking over Nicanor's declaration. 'Oh, noble legionaries! Come to save their precious armour-foundries and plunder what they can, before leaving the Forge World Principal to burn, eh?'

'I refuse to argue with you, Technoarchaeologist Land. A ship waits, hidden on the Zetek tundra. Stealth and caution are advised, and thus you will take no skimmer craft. You will make your way to Zetek via the Mesatan gearworks complex, and you will board the transport. From there you will be taken to the Ring of Iron, and onward to Terra.'

Land bares his teeth. It isn't a smile, this time. Not even a mocking one. 'I cannot leave my work unattended, Space Marine.'

The psyber-monkey hangs from a series of bars set across the laboratory's ceiling. They seem specifically constructed for the purpose. As the warrior and the scholar talk, the artificimian swings its way across the room and drops to land on its master's shoulder.

'If you remain here,' Nicanor says, 'there is a chance you will be executed by the foe. Assassins may already be on their way.'

'The Omnissiah will protect me,' Land replies, piously and sincerely making the Sign of the Cog with his linked knuckles.

'The Emperor's own Regent sent my Legion here, Arkhan Land. Perhaps *we* are the protection you speak of and pray for.'

'Meta-spiritual philosophising from a ceramite-clad brute? As if the rebellion raging across this world wasn't enough of a surprise for one lifetime! No, you Terran bastard, I am not leaving.'

Impassive to the man's resistance, Nicanor tries one last time. 'There is also a significant chance that if you are not executed by the Fabricator General's traitorous forces, you will be captured by them.'

Something – some emotion that Nicanor is incapable of

reading – flashes in the scholar's eyes. 'That is a distinct possibility,' he agrees.

'And you understand,' the warrior presses on with inhuman calm, 'that such an event cannot be allowed to transpire.'

'Ah.' Land snorts in simple disgust. 'I know too much, eh? Can't risk me defecting. Is that it?'

Nicanor says nothing. He draws his boltgun and levels it at Arkhan Land's head.

1

'He must live,' says Sigismund.

Nicanor listens to the words, words that are really an order. His raised face – and the face of every warrior present – is bathed in the flickering light of the tactical hololith. The images revolve through the air above the projection table, locked in a slow ballet of rotating illumination.

They will make planetfall in an hour. They already know everything there is to know. All that remains is to allocate landing zones, to choose which warriors will go where.

One side of the briefing display is given over to data relating to Arkhan Land.

The Arkhan Land. The explorer and scholar responsible for so many expeditions into the ancient data-crypts of Mars' crust and mantle. The man that brought back the beginnings of anti-grav technology to the nascent Imperium; the man responsible for unearthing and sharing the schematics that led to the mass-production of the Raiders and Speeders now seen in their thousands among the Legions.

Land Raiders. *Land* Speeders. The war machines are even named for him, now.

The stern, cold-eyed gaze of the Legion's First Captain falls upon Nicanor. He feels Sigismund's stare before he sees it, and when he meets his marshal's eyes, he can do nothing but nod.

'He must live,' Sigismund repeats.

Nicanor nods once. 'And he will.'

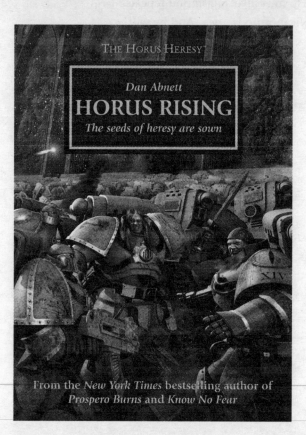

HORUS RISING
by Dan Abnett

After thousands of years of expansion and conquest, the human Imperium is at its height. His dream for humanity accomplished, the Emperor hands over the reins of power to his Warmaster, Horus, and heads back to Terra…

ABOUT THE AUTHORS

John French has written several Horus Heresy stories including the novels *Praetorian of Dorn* and *Tallarn* and the novella *The Crimson Fist*, the audio dramas *Dark Compliance*, *Templar* and *Warmaster* as well as *Agent of the Throne: Blood and Lies*. He is the author of *The Horusian Wars: Resurrection*, as well as the Ahriman series, which includes the novels *Ahriman: Exile*, *Ahriman: Sorcerer* and *Ahriman: Unchanged*, plus a number of related short stories collected in *Ahriman: Exodus*. Additionally, for the Warhammer 40,000 universe he has written the Space Marine Battles novella *Fateweaver*, plus many short stories. He lives and works in Nottingham, UK.

Josh Reynolds is the author of the Horus Heresy Primarchs novel *Fulgrim: The Palatine Phoenix*, the Warhammer 40,000 novels *Fabius Bile: Primogenitor*, *Fabius Bile: Clonelord* and *Deathstorm*, and the novellas *Hunter's Snare* and *Dante's Canyon*, along with the audio drama *Master of the Hunt*. For Warhammer Age of Sigmar he has written the novels *Eight Lamentations: Spear of Shadows*, *Hallowed Knights: Plague Garden*, *Nagash: The Undying King*, *Fury of Gork*, *Black Rift* and *Skaven Pestilens*. He has also written many stories set in the Warhammer Old World, including the End Times novels *The Return of Nagash* and *The Lord of the End Times*, the Gotrek & Felix tales *Charnel Congress*, *Road of Skulls* and *The Serpent Queen*. He lives and works in Sheffield.

David Guymer wrote the Primarchs novel *Ferrus Manus: Gorgon of Medusa*, and for Warhammer 40,000 *The Eye of Medusa* and the two The Beast Arises novels *Echoes of the Long War* and *The Last Son of Dorn*. For Warhammer Age of Sigmar he wrote the audio dramas *The Beasts of Cartha*, *Fist of Gork Fist of Mork*, *Great Red* and *Only the Faithful*. He is also the author of the Gotrek & Felix novels *Slayer*, *Kinslayer* and *City of the Damned*. He is a freelance writer and occasional scientist based in the East Riding, and was a finalist in the 2014 David Gemmell Legend Awards for his novel *Headtaker*.

Guy Haley is the author of the Horus Heresy novel *Pharos*, the Primarchs novel *Perturabo: The Hammer of Olympia* and the Warhammer 40,000 novels *Dark Imperium*, *Dante*, *Baneblade*, *Shadowsword*, *Valedor* and *Death of Integrity*. He has also written *Throneworld* and *The Beheading* for The Beast Arises series. His enthusiasm for all things greenskin has also led him to pen the eponymous Warhammer novel *Skarsnik*, as well as the End Times novel *The Rise of the Horned Rat*. He has also written stories set in the Age of Sigmar, included in *War Storm*, *Ghal Maraz* and *Call of Archaon*. He lives in Yorkshire with his wife and son.

Chris Wraight is the author of the Horus Heresy novels *Scars* and *The Path of Heaven*, the Primarchs novel *Leman Russ: The Great Wolf*, the novellas *Brotherhood of the Storm* and *Wolf King*, and the audio drama *The Sigillite*. For Warhammer 40,000 he has written *Vaults of Terra: The Carrion Throne*, *Watchers of the Throne: The Emperor's Legion*, the Space Wolves novels *Blood of Asaheim* and *Stormcaller*, and the short story collection *Wolves of Fenris*, as well as the Space Marine Battles novels *Wrath of Iron* and *Battle of the Fang*. Additionally, he has many Warhammer novels to his name, including the Time of Legends novel *Master of Dragons*, which forms part of the War of Vengeance series. Chris lives and works near Bristol, in south-west England.

Aaron Dembski-Bowden is the author of the Horus Heresy novels *The Master of Mankind*, *Betrayer* and *The First Heretic*, as well as the novella *Aurelian* and the audio drama *Butcher's Nails*, for the same series. He has also written the popular Night Lords series, the Space Marine Battles book *Helsreach*, novels *The Talon of Horus* and *Black Legion*, the Grey Knights novel *The Emperor's Gift* and numerous short stories. He lives and works in Northern Ireland.

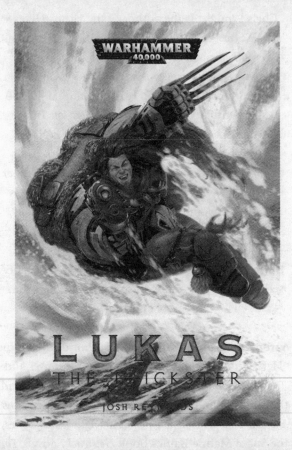

An extract from

Lukas the Trickster

Wolves howled.

Pack leaders crashed together. Avalanches of muscle and fur, sweeping together from opposite sides. Inevitable as death. Their shadows spun and fought across the walls of the *Aettergeld*, a narrow chamber of rock with high sloping walls and a massive nave set between the two halves of an immense horseshoe-shaped table.

The chamber was lit only by the glow of the firepits that ran down its centre, lambent shadows crowding the edges as if trying to creep away from those of the combatants. Ancient battle-banners hung from the ceiling, rippling in the intense heat. Weapons and other, less obvious trophies marked the roughly carved walls. Cheers and whistles pierced the air. The benches were packed and *mjod* flowed freely.

Naturally, there was an audience. Wolves didn't have secrets from each other. At least, not that they would admit.

Lukas the Trickster sat well back from all the excitement, near the largest of the firepits that dotted the chamber. He leaned on a massive wolf, idly scratching it between the ears. 'Who do you think it'll be, then?' He glanced down at the wolf. The great beast grunted and made to roll over, uninterested in conversation. Lukas chuckled and set his legs across the back of another wolf.

He leaned back amid the massive hairy bodies that lay about him in untidy piles. The smell of wet fur and animal musk enveloped him. In the close environs of the chamber, that smell wasn't unpleasant, but it was impossible to ignore. There were a dozen or more sleeping wolves around him, a full pack. The brutes often sought the warmth of the Aett in the colder seasons, where meat and water were freely available as well. Wolves were opportunists at heart – it was one of the reasons Lukas enjoyed their company.

'You are most hospitable companions, for all that you smell awful,' he said, turning to study the ancient banners and battle-worn trophies hanging from the walls. Since the setting of the Fang's roots, the Aettergeld had been used as a place of judgement and sentencing. Sven Ironhand had declared his exile here, and Garn Felltooth had bared his throat to the Great Wolf's axe. Disputes were weighed, blood-prices paid and the guilty condemned. It was a place of debts owed and restitutions made.

Lukas had been in this chamber a hundred times before, and would be a hundred times more before his thread was at last severed by Morkai's jaws. That was his wyrd, and he was content in it. He was a sour note in the song of heroes, a fact he prided himself on. Of what possible interest was a perfect song? Better to be interesting than perfect.

Lukas knew he was many things – lazy, disrespectful, often unhygienic – but never boring. He was the only man living who had killed a doppelgangrel by hand, and the only warrior to ever have taken a punch from Berek Thunderfist and remain standing.

He was the Jackalwolf. The Strifeson. The Laughing One. The Trickster. The warriors of the Rout collected names the way a child might collect shells. Each name came with a story, a saga of heroism or foolishness. Sometimes both. Every warrior was a collection of stories, with the same beginning and only one end.

A roar went up from the gathered Wolf Guard as one of the combatants was sent rolling through a firepit. The warrior leapt to his feet and tore his burning shirt from his frame. Even un-armoured, the strength of the fighters was such that they could burst stone and warp metal. One ill-timed blow and a Great Company would be electing a new Wolf Lord before the day was out.

Benches had been upended in the struggle. Braziers spilled crackling embers across the floor, and a rug made from the slick pelt of a sea troll was burning. In the centre of the chamber, the two mighty figures came together again, snarling and cursing. The gathered huscarls stomped their feet, adding thunder to the storm.

Helwinter had come round at last, and it was time for the Jackalwolf to find a new pack. Or, rather, for a new pack to be burdened with the Jackalwolf. The jarls drew sticks until only two remained. Then, as was tradition, those two would beat each other bloody until one yielded. A simple procedure, and an entertaining one.

Lukas felt a faint vibration as the storm outside lashed at the mountain. The few lumens in the hall flickered. No one noticed, preoccupied as they were by the sight of two Wolf Lords pummelling each other into bloody surrender. The two warriors were of a similar size and bulk, giants among giants. Leathery faces tanned by glare and hardened by age rippled in savage snarls. Distended jaw lines bulged as fangs snapped.

Yellow eyes glared with kill-lust. The other jarls circled the combatants, shouting encouragement.

Not all of them were in attendance on this momentous occasion. He knocked on a wolf's head with his knuckle. 'No sign of my old sparring partners, Hrothgar Ironblade or Berek Thunderfist. Gunnar Red Moon is in hiding. And Egil Iron-Wolf is nowhere in sight, which is something of a relief, if I'm being honest.' Part of Lukas dreaded the day he would be foisted on that pack. The smell of machine oil alone would kill him.

'No sign of the Great Wolf either. Of course, while Grimnar often boasts of sharing the burdens of duty with his subordinates, he has ever avoided this one.' Lukas snorted and ran his hand through the crimson tangles of his beard. 'Given that he was the one who made it a tradition, maybe he's exempt – or maybe he has simply had a bellyful of me.'

The absences left only a few familiar faces. Engir Krakendoom, obviously. Lukas paid little attention to his current jarl. Despite his best efforts, he looked like a condemned man on the cusp of reprieve, something Lukas took as a compliment.

From where he sat, he could hear the wagers that flew fast between the huscarls, weighing the merits of both warriors. Kjarl Grimblood was the older, his slate grey hair and beard whipping about as he drove a crushing blow against the side of his opponent's skull. Bran Redmaw staggered, but replied in kind almost instantly. His mane of hair stood up stiff on his scalp, and his veins bulged like tension cables. He champed his teeth spasmodically as he struck Grimblood again and again, pummelling him.

'You are the one who can see the future, Grimblood,' Redmaw roared, his words echoing through the chamber. 'You know how this ends.'

'The future the fire showed me wasn't this one,' Grimblood

snarled. His big fists, scarred and gnarled, struck like pistons, matching his opponent blow for blow. 'He isn't my wyrd, not this season. Take him and be damned!'

'If I were not used to it, I might be insulted,' Lukas murmured to one of the wolves. The beast yawned at him, and he scratched it behind the ears. 'Still, that too is tradition, and who am I to gainsay it, eh?' The wolf didn't reply. Then, they never did. Another reason he preferred their company to that of his brothers. Lukas chuckled as Grimblood struck Redmaw a resounding blow. 'Another hit like that, and the decision is made.'

Lukas was interested to see who would win this time. Who would he be this season? 'Not all Wolf Lords need a Jackalwolf,' he said, idly stroking one of the wolves. 'Some are in want of a Laughing One. Others need the Strifeson. Different faces for different places.' The wolf passed gas and kicked gently, showing what it thought of that. Lukas waved a hand in front of him, trying to disperse the smell. 'You still smell better than Iron-Wolf.'

Lukas was many stories tangled together, and the one he told depended on the audience. For Krakendoom, he had played the part of instigator and agitator, shaking his self-satisfied warriors out of a long complacency. What part he would play in the coming season depended on who lost the fight.

Redmaw snatched up a bench, scattering those members of the Wolf Guard who had been sitting on it. He struck Grimblood with it, hurling him to the floor in a cloud of splinters. Grimblood groaned and rolled over, spitting blood. He sat up and waved Redmaw away as the other jarl stalked towards him. 'Enough, brother. Enough. I can feel my brains sloshing in my skull from that last hit.'

'Do you yield, then?' Redmaw demanded.

'Aye, I do. Give me a moment – the world is spinning.' Grim-blood accepted a helping hand from one of the other jarls and was hauled to his feet. He tenderly probed his jaw. 'I yield,' he said more formally.

Redmaw thrust his fist up, and those warriors loyal to him began to cheer louder still and slam their fists on the table. Redmaw looked at the other Wolf Lords. 'You heard him. I win. The Jackalwolf is his burden for the coming season.' Lukas frowned, resolving to stick something unpleasant in Redmaw's mjod when next the opportunity presented itself.

'It is done, then,' Engir Krakendoom said. Dark of skin and temperament alike, the Krakendoom had a voice as deep as the seas. 'He is your burden now, the way he has been mine, and Goresson's before me.' He gestured to Finn Goresson. The other Wolf Lord was tattooed from head to toe and stank of bear grease and weapon oil. He tugged on the crimson braid of his beard and narrowed his amber eyes.

'Aye, and you're welcome to the bastard.'

'My thanks, brother,' Grimblood spat. Lukas almost laughed to see his expression. He restrained himself, though. Best to let tempers cool.